Welcome to the January 2009 collection of Harlequin Presents!

This month be sure to catch the second installment of Lynne Graham's trilogy VIRGIN BRIDES, ARROGANT HUSBANDS with her new book, *The Ruthless Magnate's Virgin Mistress*. Jessica goes from office cleaner to the billionaire boss's mistress in Sharon Kendrick's *Bought for the Sicilian Billionaire's Bed*, and sexual attraction simmers uncontrollably when Tara has to face the ruthless count in *Count Maxime's Virgin* by Susan Stephens. You'll be whisked off to the Mediterranean in Michelle Reid's *The Greek's Forced Bride*, and in Jennie Lucas's *Italian Prince, Wedlocked Wife*, innocent Lucy tries to resist the seductive ways of Prince Maximo. A ruthless tycoon will stop at nothing to bed his convenient wife in Anne McAllister's *Antonides' Forbidden Wife*, and friends become lovers when playboy Alex Richardson needs a bride in Kate Hardy's *Hotly Bedded, Conveniently Wedded*. Plus, in Trish Wylie's *Claimed by the Rogue Billionaire*, attraction reaches the boiling point between Gabe and Ash, but can either of them forget the past?

We'd love to hear what you think about Presents. E-mail us at Presents@hmb.co.uk or join in the discussions at www.iheartpresents.com and www.sensationalromance.blogspot.com, where you'll also find more information about books and authors!

Virgin BRIDES ♥ Arrogant HUSBANDS

Demure but defiant…
Can three international playboys
tame their disobedient brides?

Lysander, the gorgeous, dynamic
Greek tycoon…

Nikolai, the ruthless, charismatic
Russian magnate…

Leandro, the sexy, aristocratic
Spanish billionaire…

Proud, masculine and passionate, these men are
used to having it all. But enter Ophelia, Abbey and
Molly, three feisty virgins to whom wealth and
power mean little. In stories filled with drama,
desire and secrets of the past, find out how these
arrogant men capture the hearts of these women.

The Greek Tycoon's Disobedient Bride,
December 2008

The Ruthless Magnate's Virgin Mistress,
January 2009

The Spanish Billionaire's Pregnant Wife,
February 2009

Lynne Graham
THE RUTHLESS MAGNATE'S VIRGIN MISTRESS

BRIDES ♥ HUSBANDS

HARLEQUIN®

TORONTO • NEW YORK • LONDON
AMSTERDAM • PARIS • SYDNEY • HAMBURG
STOCKHOLM • ATHENS • TOKYO • MILAN • MADRID
PRAGUE • WARSAW • BUDAPEST • AUCKLAND

ISBN-13: 978-0-373-12787-0
ISBN-10:   0-373-12787-1

THE RUTHLESS MAGNATE'S VIRGIN MISTRESS

First North American Publication 2009.

Copyright © 2008 by Lynne Graham.

This is a work of fiction. Names, characters, places and incidents are either the product of the author's imagination or are used fictitiously, and any resemblance to actual persons, living or dead, business establishments, events or locales is entirely coincidental.

This edition published by arrangement with Harlequin Books S.A.

® and TM are trademarks of the publisher. Trademarks indicated with ® are registered in the United States Patent and Trademark Office, the Canadian Trade Marks Office and in other countries.

www.eHarlequin.com

Printed in U.S.A.

All about the author...
Lynne Graham

Of Irish/Scottish parentage, LYNNE GRAHAM has
lived in Northern Ireland all her life. She has one
brother. She grew up in a seaside village and now
lives in a country house surrounded by a woodland
garden, which is wonderfully private.

Lynne first met her husband when she was fourteen.
They married after she completed a degree at
Edinburgh University. Lynne wrote her first book at
fifteen and it was rejected everywhere. She started
writing again when she was home with her first
child. It took several attempts before she sold her
first book, and the delight of seeing that book for sale
in the local newsagents has never been forgotten.

Lynne always wanted a large family, and she has five
children. Her eldest and her only natural child is in
her twenties and is a university graduate. Her other
children, who are every bit as dear to her heart, are
adopted: two from Sri Lanka and two from Guatemala.
In Lynne's home, there is a rich and diverse cultural
mix, which adds a whole extra dimension of interest
and discovery to family life.

The family has two pets. Thomas, a very large and
affectionate black cat, bosses the dog and hunts
rabbits. The dog is Daisy, an adorable but not very
bright West Highland white terrier, who loves being
chased by the cat. At night, dog and cat sleep together
in front of the kitchen stove.

Lynne loves gardening and cooking, collects
everything from old toys to rock specimens and is
crazy about every aspect of Christmas.

PROLOGUE

THE setting was a grand mansion in the most prestigious area of St Petersburg, its soaring majestic windows giving exclusive views across the Fontanka River. The enormous room was packed in the aftermath of a memorial service, yet many of the guests had not even known the departed. The lure that had brought them was the towering presence of Nikolai Danilovich Arlov, the oil magnate, whose vast wealth was the stuff of legend.

Indifferent as always to being the centre of attention, Nikolai was heavily engaged in a business phone-call. A tall, powerful figure, with cropped black hair and eyes as dark and hard as rain-washed stone, he was a breathtakingly handsome man with a smouldering sexual charisma that radiated masculinity. Women watched him with unhidden hunger, while his minders and aides studiously screened him from every possible approach. Few of those present received more than a distant nod from their host. But many would dine out for weeks on the social cachet of having been a guest in his jaw-droppingly fantastic home.

Nikolai ignored virtually everyone. As tough as an Arctic winter and as relentless as a juggernaut, he was a maverick who played by his own rules. He loathed time-wasters and tedious social events. It was the pursuit of power and profit that energised and drove him. He had attended his late father's memorial service purely as a matter of form, for close connections of the family kind were utterly unknown to him. He could not even recall when he had last spoken to the old man. His father had hated and resented him almost from the day of his birth and his two older half-brothers feared and envied their fabulously successful sibling. However, neither of those undisputed facts had prevented Nikolai's relatives from begging him to take charge of the dead man's tangled affairs and ensure that the estate was settled without cost or inconvenience to themselves. It had not once occurred to them that Nikolai might have a more private and personal motivation for agreeing to carry out that thankless task.

When a dazzling blond beauty in a power suit appeared in a doorway invisible tension surged through Nikolai's lean, powerful frame, but it lasted only for a split second. His classic, high, carved cheekbones might have been chipped out of solid bronze. One glance at Sveta's expression told him that she was the bringer of bad news and that the questions that had plagued him as a child were to remain unanswered: the search of his father's personal effects had proved fruitless.

'Nothing.' Frustration and annoyance laced Sveta's low-pitched voice when she drew level with him. Like her colleagues, Olya and Darya, she was a high achiever, never satisfied with anything less than positive results.

'*Nichivo*—no problem.' His tone was one of dismissal and as he spoke, so he believed. He saw no reason why the mystery of his exact parentage should keep him awake at night. All the documents his father had left behind had now been examined; safes had been opened, desks emptied, deposit boxes tracked down. What had appeared to be a promising opportunity had failed to deliver even a jot of new information. He didn't know the name of his mother and he didn't know where or why he had been born. And now he most probably never would.

But so what? Nikolai asked himself with a mental shrug. Such paltry facts were irrelevant to a male who had always known who he was and where he was going. At the age of thirty-three he had realised his every ambition a thousand times over. He had nothing to apologise for and nobody to impress. Investigating his maternal ancestry was a waste of valuable time and energy.

At the precise moment that Nikolai reached that conclusion a commotion was breaking out at the lower end of the room. Heads were turning to a buzz of excited comment. A frown was indenting his brow even before he was informed that his current lover, Brigitta Jansen, had just made her entrance. She had flown in from Paris without an invitation. Cold displeasure gripped him because he considered her arrival as that of a gatecrasher and an intrusion on his privacy. A smile on her flawless face, the Dutch movie actress walked towards him, basking in the attention she was attracting.

Fifteen minutes later, Nikolai was on his way to the airport alone. He had left Brigitta in hysterics, surrounded by her sycophantic staff of hangers-on. If her intent had been to make him feel guilty for ditching her, she had failed abysmally. Emotional blackmail was no more to his taste than feminine demands or the suggestion that he might be anything other than a single guy, free to sample other company and other beds as and when he liked.

He wondered why he always landed bunny-boilers who started out cool and calm but speedily went into the pursuit mode of deadly missiles. He told no lies; he was direct about what he wanted. Sex was as necessary to his health and comfort as food. It had nothing to do with the mythical L word that women flung as an excuse to try to change the ground rules. Love wasn't in his vocabulary. Why was something as basic and simple as sex a continual flashpoint for trouble? Perturbed by that unprecedented train of philosophical thought and by the dark mood he was determined not to acknowledge, he took another business call with alacrity.

An hour after dining on his private jet, Nikolai left Sveta and her colleagues at work and went for a shower. Fifteen minutes later, he answered the knock on the bedroom door with only a towel wrapped round his lean bronzed hips. His black brows drew together in astonishment when Sveta walked in. Her suit had vanished and her remarkable body was now embellished only by an apricot silk corset-and-knicker set. 'What the hell—?'

'Please don't say anything until I've finished, sir. Olya, Darya and I thought that you might be in the mood to be distracted,' Sveta murmured softly.

Olya, a voluptuous brunette, strolled in, wearing a similar outfit in emerald green. 'You've had a tricky week. A little down time in the right female company could help you to relax.'

Darya, the third of his aides, her platinum-blond hair cut razor-short above her strikingly attractive face, entered sporting turquoise lace lingerie and struck a provocative pose. 'We know what you need. We also believe that we can deliver. Choose one of us and there will be no repercussions, emotional or otherwise.'

His hard, handsome face unrevealing, Nikolai studied the three women and wondered why on earth he had assumed that there was safety in numbers. No repercussions? Who did they think they were kidding? As sharp as blades in the intelligence stakes and as effective in business as sharks in a wildlife pond, each of them was ferociously loyal to him. No man could have equalled their single-minded devotion to his interests. And like him they never forgot what they came from.

'But if you feel that one-to-one might be too personal or divisive to team spirit...' Sveta leant back against the door to close it with her shapely derriere and gave him an understanding smile '...we have no objection to sharing you and every expectation that you will rise to the challenge.'

CHAPTER ONE

'YOU look amazing,' Sally, the beautician, chattered as she fanned out Abbey's unruly mane of flame-coloured curls over her slim shoulders. 'You're going to be the star tonight.'

Abbey seriously doubted that forecast and reckoned that only a woman confident of her face and body would actually want to take part in a fashion show. She was only there by default, stepping in last minute for the amateur model who had twisted her knee in a fall during the dress rehearsal. Abbey had never liked either her face or her body. When she was a child the mirror had been her enemy, destroying her every dream of being a fairy princess in disguise.

One of her earliest memories had been of hearing her father complain that she was an ugly duckling. Sadly for her, however, the swan phase had failed to transpire, Abbey reflected wryly. Her hair had stayed defiantly red, her freckles had increased and her elongated gawky legs had continued to ensure that she towered over most people at a comfortable five feet nine inches in her bare feet. In her opinion, her unfashionably large breasts and hips only increased her oddness. Only once in her life had Abbey considered herself blessed by any claim to attraction. That had been the miraculous day when Jeffrey Carmichael had asked her out. During the months that had run up to their wedding day the world had truly seemed to be a joyous place sprinkled with stardust and happiness. But even Jeffrey had once suggested that she might look better as a blonde.

'Caroline is incredible,' Sally commented as a fair-haired woman in a wheelchair sped busily past. 'I really do admire her. To have lost so much and still be so keen to help others.'

'That's Caroline all over,' Abbey agreed as she admired her brother's wife equally. Caroline might have lost the power of her legs six years earlier, but she still cared for her husband and two children, met the demands of a full-time job and made room for fund-raising activities to support Futures, the spinal injuries charity that had helped her in her hour of need. The fashion show that Abbey had helped to organise was being held in aid of Futures.

'Someone told me that she got hurt in a car crash on her brother's wedding day…'

'Yes,' Abbey confirmed, her freckles standing out against her sudden pallor. 'A drunk driver.'

'I'm sure I read about it in the newspaper at the time.'

'There was a lot of press coverage.' Abbey did not want to think back to what had happened to the wedding party that dark, wet October day. One moment she'd had everything to live for, the next nothing, but she knew how lucky she was to have emerged virtually unscathed from the wreckage. Her brother's life had been torn apart and, although the pessimistic had forecast otherwise, his marriage had survived the cruel blow that Caroline had suffered.

'Love the make-up, Sally,' Caroline remarked, wheeling to a halt beside them. 'You've done Abbey proud.'

'It wasn't difficult. She's got great bones and eyes.'

'You look wonderful,' Caroline told her sister-in-law warmly.

Abbey studied her reflection. She thought she looked outrageous with her violet-coloured eyes smothered in exotic plum shades and glitter and diamante shimmering in an artistic arc across her cheekbones, but she supposed that the spectacular heavy make-up was all part and parcel of the illusion of glamour. 'Is Drew here yet?' she enquired.

Caroline's face shadowed. 'No. He was still at the office when I called.'

Abbey felt Caroline's disappointment and wondered what her brother was playing at. Nobody had worked harder than Caroline to get this show on the road and she deserved for her husband to take respectful notice of her achievement. But, then, the family concierge business, Support Systems, had recently moved to upmarket premises in Knightsbridge and hired more staff, substantially increasing overheads. As a result, all of them were working longer hours and dealing with more clients. Abbey adored the busyness and variety of her job. Customers hired them to take care of everything they could not find the time to do for themselves—wide-ranging tasks that ran from walking the dog and picking up dry cleaning to booking holidays, shopping for presents and finding domestic staff and repairmen.

It was all a far cry from the life her snobbish sexist father would have chosen for her. He had refused to allow her to go to university or to train for a profession. Abbey remained painfully aware that, next to her brother, she had been a nobody in her father's eyes. The older man had often treated his only daughter as an irritation and a disappointment. In fact only on the day Abbey married Jeffrey had her father looked at her with approval and pride as if marriage to a successful man was her biggest achievement.

'You look like the Queen in *Snow White*,' her niece, Alice, whispered, big eyes fixed in fascination to her aunt's face.

'The baddie who thought she was gorgeous and cracked the magic mirror she was always talking to?' Abbey groaned.

'She may have been bad but she was really beautiful,' Alice lisped.

'Watch your face,' Sally warned when Abbey bent down to hug the six-year-old with easy affection. Across the room, Alice's twin brother, Benjamin, was as usual fully engrossed in a book. Abbey was very close to her brother's children. After the car accident she had moved in with the family to help out while Caroline was undergoing an intensive physiotherapy programme. She had soon discovered that the children's needs and her own unrelenting grief had been best met by keeping busy for as many hours of the day as possible.

Nerves were making Abbey as tense as an overstretched piece of elastic. Sally removed the protective cape she wore and Abbey got up to go and peer out at the audience from behind the curtains that shielded the catwalk from the dressing area. 'I don't know why I agreed to do this,' she muttered.

'Because it's for a good cause,' Caroline piped up cheerfully at her elbow. 'And all our lucky stars came out tonight. Guess who's out here?'

'One of the A-list celebrities you invited?' Abbey guessed.

'Nikolai Danilovich Arlov.'

'Who?'

'For goodness' sake, Abbey. You've got to know who *he* is! Only a Russian billionaire—'

'The one whose vigorous sex life is always giving the tabloids headlines and centre spreads?' As Caroline gave a reluctant nod of confirmation Abbey grimaced. 'The guy's only one step removed from a barnyard animal. He's sleaze personified.'

'His donation will still be welcome. Don't be so judgemental, Abbey,' her brother's wife scolded. 'Rich single men always have loads of girlfriends—'

'He always picks sluts willing to spill all their bedroom secrets in print for a hefty payment. It tells you all you need to know about him—'

'That the poor guy is a target for the greediest and most unscrupulous gold-diggers in town?'

'Are you talking about Nikolai Arlov?' Sally chimed in. 'He's been on his mobile phone ever since he arrived. He is absolutely gorgeous. If I got the chance to sleep with him I'd want to kiss and tell as well!'

Caroline giggled. 'Are you serious?'

'I'd be proud to tell the world that I had caught his eye,' the beautician insisted. 'And according to what I've read about his generosity, it would be well worth my while to be one of his harem.'

'Men like that are just users,' Abbey opined in disgust.

'What would you know about men like that?' her sister-in-law queried drily. 'When were you last out on a date?'

'You know when,' Abbey reminded her.

'Was it the guy who spent the whole evening talking about his ex-wife and confiding that he still loved her?' Caroline groaned.

'He had tears in his eyes when he told me,' Abbey completed and peered out at the audience. 'Where is the billionaire seated?'

'You can't miss him. He's right at the end of the runway with a sizeable entourage—three beauties ministering to his every need and two massive minders hovering over him.' Sally shared that extraneous information with enthusiasm.

'The paparazzi are waiting outside for him. Just having Nikolai Arlov in the building is a major coup,' Caroline declared with satisfaction. 'Thanks to him, Futures will get valuable free publicity.'

'At least he's useful for something other than selling tacky tabloids,' Abbey declared as the avant-garde designer of the fashion collection moved to the podium and the music switched to the intro and the opening speech. She peered down the runway but it was no good: her long-distance eyesight wasn't good enough. All she could see was a big dark man with two dazzling young women hanging over him like attentive waitresses. The first model sashayed down the runway to a chorus of appreciative applause. Pale at the prospect of her approaching debut, Abbey moved out of the way of the models lining up to await their turn.

Many models had featured in Nikolai's bed, but that did not mean he had garnered any interest in fashion. Business calls were a welcome release from boredom while he waited for the show to begin. But the very leggy redhead who appeared half an hour into the show was so sensationally beautiful that Nikolai actually forgot what he was talking about on the phone. He didn't know what it was about her, but he took one look and he wanted her with an immediacy and an urgency he hadn't experienced in years. Her mesmerising smoky eyes reflected the dense purple-blue of the amethyst pendant someone had cleverly fixed round her throat. Her bone structure was striking, unforgettable. She was all woman from her head of fabulous Titian curls to the swell of her voluptuous breasts and generous hips. A shimmering dark blue evening gown showcased her luscious curves and lent her the theatrical allure of a thirties movie star.

'I want to meet her after the show,' he told Sveta without hesitation. 'Find out who she is.'

Abbey simply thought Nikolai was the most beautiful man she had ever seen. He had stunning eyes, cheekbones sharp enough to cut diamonds and a gorgeous wide, shapely mouth. Whatever, one glance and she felt utterly overwhelmed by that amazing combination of purely superficial attributes, her heart thumping inside her like a road drill and her mouth as dry as a bone. She was shocked rigid by her response, for she had always believed she was more cerebral than physical. She didn't know what drew her to him beyond the obvious. It was as though his precise arrangement of features executed some sort of spellbinding effect on her and her wits took a hike, for when she looked once at his bold bronzed features she found she had to look again and again and again and at length to satisfy her indecent craving to see him.

Sveta murmured, 'She's married. She's wearing a ring.'

Nikolai never slept with other men's wives. It was one of the very few embargos he respected: he gave married women a very wide berth. 'Check it out,' he urged, unwilling to credit that she might be out of reach, as it was rare for anything to be unconquerable for Nikolai; there were always ways and means of acquiring what he wanted. And his senses were already humming at the prospect of entertaining the redhead in his bed that night, unveiling those magnificent breasts and endless long legs for his private enjoyment. He remembered the way her glittering gaze had lingered on him and had no doubt that his interest was returned. If she was a wife she was an unfaithful one.

One of the dressers began to strip the evening gown from Abbey and assist her at speed into her next outfit. Another removed her jewellery. Her skin felt clammy and she felt dizzy. What had happened to her out there? Men didn't have that big an effect on Abbey. Her nature was cool rather than passionate. Jeffrey was the only man she had ever wanted and she had fallen for him in her teens, moving from an explosive adolescent infatuation to deep joyous love with continued exposure to his company. There had never been anyone else for her and only loneliness and the fear that she might be acting a little obsessively had persuaded her, with Caroline's encouragement, to try dating other men over the past year. All those dates had been non-starters, for none of those men had had an ounce of Jeffrey's intelligence or natural charm.

Caroline joined her sister-in-law while the younger woman's make-up was being touched up. 'Nikolai Arlov has asked for your phone number!' she announced.

'He can't have it,' Abbey replied without hesitation as her arms were guided into a shirt and her legs into wide-legged trousers. A fashionable tan raincoat was fed into place over both garments and the belt cinched to accentuate her narrow waist. What did she have to say to a Russian billionaire with a notorious reputation with her sex? Absolutely nothing.

'But you will at least *speak* to him?' Caroline pressed anxiously. 'We can't afford to offend the guy. Think of Futures' funds, Abbey.'

Abbey could not help resenting that piece of advice, for she could see no reason why she should be forced to speak to a man she didn't want to speak to. And then all of a sudden she remembered how she had looked at him minutes earlier and felt guiltily that her behaviour might well have prompted him to make an approach.

'Okay. Drew here yet?'

'Not yet,' the blond woman responded ruefully.

'He's obsessed with work right now,' Abbey proffered as an excuse.

'As long as that's all that's keeping him out late so many nights,' Caroline quipped, startling Abbey.

'For goodness' sake, Drew adores you!' Abbey countered.

'He's been rather evasive and quiet on the adoration front recently. But, no, I don't think there's another woman,' Caroline confirmed, meeting Abbey's anxious gaze in the mirror. 'I don't think he's got the time or the energy to neglect *two* of us!'

Abbey relaxed again, but she hadn't missed the thread of annoyance and worry in her sister-in-law's voice and she resolved to have a word with her brother for his thoughtlessness. What on earth was Drew playing at? Did he really work this late often? Didn't he appreciate that Caroline needed his support and company at home? Abbey refused to work after eight in the evening unless there was a crisis; she usually went into the office very early in the morning and it was impossible to burn the candle at both ends and stay healthy. At night she liked to go home via the gym where she exercised, and then cook a light supper and chill out before bedtime.

'A billionaire wants to ask you out and you're not even shaking!' Sally censured. 'Aren't you excited?'

'Why would I be? He's extremely handsome, but what would we have in common?' Abbey asked.

'I want you to go out with him just so that you can tell me what it was like,' the beautician confided. 'Are you going to speak to him after the show?'

'Seems like I don't have much choice.' But when Abbey thought about Nikolai Arlov's wonderfully dark deep-set eyes her stomach contracted. She questioned her susceptibility, disturbed by the nervous tension licking through her like a forest fire. She felt as though she didn't know herself any more. And when she sashayed down the catwalk again, his intense gaze didn't stray from her for a single second. She avoided looking in his direction to the best of her ability but, in an odd way that she didn't want to think about, she liked his unwavering attention.

'You should borrow something to wear for the supper afterwards. After all the glam outfits you've paraded in front of him it won't do to appear in the jeans and T-shirt you arrived in,' Caroline opined.

'My own clothes will do fine.'

Her sister-in-law caught her narrow wrist between her fingers before she turned away. 'Don't blow Arlov away. You can't mourn my brother for ever.'

Why not? Abbey almost demanded. Jeffrey was dead and that *would* last for ever. In the same way she knew she would miss her husband for ever and never forget him. She didn't think she would ever get over losing the love of her life and she wasn't ashamed of that fact. Love like that was precious, a great deal more precious than anything she had been offered since her husband's death had left her a widow. She was not stupid. She was all too well aware that most men only thought of one thing when they looked at her large breasts and long legs. Ironically that one thing had been the very last thing on Jeffrey's mind, she conceded wryly.

Nikolai was not surprised to find Abbey Carmichael waiting for him at the buffet held after the show. But he *was* taken aback by her make-up-bare face and casual apparel, since women usually went to a great deal more effort in the glamour stakes when he was around. In actuality she could get away with the scrubbed natural look because her creamy freckled skin had the sun-warmed glow of a peach and she simply looked younger and more fragile with her glorious fiery hair tumbling casually round her narrow shoulders.

Caroline and Futures' charity director greeted the Russian tycoon and began to talk to him. Abbey sipped her glass of wine and studied the tall black-haired Russian, wondering why his obvious boredom should set her teeth on edge. No doubt he performed miracles with his money, but he didn't necessarily have to have a personal interest in the charities that benefited from his generosity. She was conscious that his attention was on her, not on his companions. Her bra felt tight when she breathed and her breasts tingled with awareness inside the lace cups. Minutes later, Abbey was beckoned over and introduced.

'Abbey Carmichael…Nikolai Danilovich Arlov…'

CHAPTER TWO

NIKOLAI held on to Abbey's slim hand longer than was necessary and commented as he walked her away, 'You're the most beautiful woman here tonight.'

'I'm flattered that you noticed me when you were so busy with your phone,' Abbey murmured tongue-in-cheek, embarrassingly aware of the way his gaze was welded to her generous mouth. She wondered what it would feel like to kiss him and startled herself with the thought.

Ignoring the potential sting of that comment, Nikolai smiled while Caroline shot the younger woman a warning glance. 'I'm afraid that business dominates my life. Let me buy the blue dress for you. It would be a sin if it was bought and worn by any other woman.'

Shock at that careless offer made Abbey's lips part company and she blinked in surprise. 'No, thanks, Mr Arlov. I prefer to buy my own clothes.'

'Nikolai,' he urged, watching her for the response he was accustomed to receiving from her sex.

Meeting his stunning dark eyes head-on, she felt extraordinarily short of breath and her tummy flipped. He had astonishingly long and luxuriant black eyelashes for a man. Her nipples had tightened into stinging hardness and she was terrified they would show through her cotton T-shirt. She folded her arms hurriedly. She had never been so conscious of her own body or of a man's proximity in her entire life and the level of that awareness was unnerving her. 'I don't think I know you well enough—'

'A situation which I am eager to remedy,' he cut in, smooth as glass. 'Would you like to go to a club when this affair winds up? Or perhaps for a meal?'

'No, I'll be winding up, too. I have to get up for work in the morning,' Abbey pointed out in a flat, discouraging tone.

Exasperated dark as ebony eyes rested on her mutinous face. 'Are you always this difficult to pin down for a date?'

'I'm just not interested in getting to know you any better,' Abbey told him honestly. 'Don't waste your time on me.'

Blunt rejection was not an occurrence that Nikolai was familiar with. Women usually went out of their way to attract his attention and hold it. His gifts were received with shrieks of pleasure and gratitude, not ignored or refused. To be turned down by a woman who did not even try to sound regretful was a novel experience for him and not one he savoured.

'I allow nobody to waste my time. Tell me, do you continue to wear a wedding ring to keep other men at a distance?'

Abbey could not credit his insolence in daring to ask her that question. Did his choice of words suggest that he was already aware that she was a widow? If anything Nikolai Danilovich Arlov was proving to be even more obnoxious than she had expected him to be, she ac-

knowledged, her pride still smarting from his imperti-
nent offer to buy her the blue evening gown. She glanced
down at the familiar band of gold on her wedding finger.
'No, I still wear my wedding ring to remind me that I
was once married to a very special man.'

Rare anger sparked and flared through Nikolai. He
breathed in slow and deep. The defiant tilt of her chin,
her patronising tone and the haughty look in her eyes
offended his pride and masculinity. But more than
anything else he did not want to hear her say such things.
He wanted her to be carefree and hot as he was for a
more intimate acquaintance, not some idealistic clean-
living widow who had buried her heart in the grave with
her Mr Perfect husband. Keen to steer the conversation
to other channels, he asked her where she worked.

Abbey told him with pride that she was a partner in
a concierge business with her brother.

'The service industry is booming at present,' he
remarked, and he asked her how she had got involved
in devoting her spare time to a spinal injuries charity.
She explained that Caroline was married to her brother
and described the very real support given by Futures
during the challenging transition the blond woman had
had to make from being able-bodied and independent
to disabled.

'Like a lot of people in the same position her whole
life changed and she didn't know where to turn,' Abbey
advanced with enthusiasm, for she was happier to talk
about the charity than talk about herself. 'She could no
longer do the job she had trained for—she was a chef
and a good one. Her home wasn't adapted to her needs
and she had financial problems because the accident put
paid to her earnings. Futures stepped in with advice,

counselling and a grant that covered her most pressing requirements—'

'You're a good advocate for the work that Futures does. If I offer to make a large donation to the charity, will that buy me some of your precious time?'

Abbey was stunned by the staggering concept of anyone purchasing her time and company with cash. Hot colour washed her cheeks, her violet eyes widening in disbelief. 'I'm not a hooker for hire, Mr Danilovich.'

He rested his brilliant dark eyes on her. 'I believe I'm already aware of that fact. But like most keen business-men I will use any angle that works to get me what I want. If your heart is softened by the prospect of the charity benefiting from my interest in you, I will not be slow to take advantage of it. Do you want to talk figures?'

'No, I do not!' Abbey gasped, shocked to the core by his attitude. Only when heads turned in their radius did she realise that her sharp tone had carried farther afield. In receipt of curious glances, she flushed. 'If you wish to make a donation, please make sure it has nothing to do with me. You should discuss it with Cyril Townsend, Futures' director.'

'But it will have *everything* to do with you. At least let me take you home, *lubimaya*,' he breathed, his Russian accent curling richly round the vowel sounds.

Abbey intercepted a pleading look from her sister-in-law and compressed her lips. She was reluctant to embarrass the blond woman by offending the charity's VIP guest. 'I'm afraid not. I'm driving my sister-in-law home,' she confided.

In receipt of yet another rebuff, Nikolai studied her as if he could not believe his ears. 'Then when *will* I see you again?'

'I don't think a second meeting is on the agenda,' Abbey replied.

'I want you.'

I want you. That admission was bold and uncompromising and he delivered it like a challenge, a sworn statement of intent. Her heart lurched inside her ribcage as he stared down at her with stubborn brooding force etched in his lean, sardonic face. He had buckets of sex appeal and, no matter how hard she tried, she was insanely aware of his breathtaking good looks and far from impervious to his rough-edged masculine appeal. Antipathy and resentment shot through her tall shapely body, however, and she lifted her chin. 'I'm not for sale, Mr Danilovich. And I can't be bribed.'

'Every human being under the sun has a price. It may not be money, it may be something else. It doesn't follow that a bribe, as you call it, is morally wrong if it wins positive results,' Nikolai traded.

'We don't see the world the same way,' Abbey countered drily, unsurprised by his attempt to package his unacceptable bribe into an excusable act of benevolence. She was dealing with a hard, cynical man whose greatest god was money and who did not know how to accept the word *no* when it conflicted with his wishes. 'And I doubt that we ever will.'

'I'm a realist and rarely wrong.'

'How comforting it must be to see oneself as supreme in all fields,' Abbey replied.

'Apparently not in this encounter,' he quipped.

'Goodbye, Mr Arlov. I hope you won't regard a donation to Futures as being in any way influenced by my behaviour.' Abbey walked away from him with a strong sense of relief.

Nikolai watched her until she vanished from view. He felt angry and frustrated. He had never met a more annoying or intriguing woman and her unexpected resistance and prickly personality had only heightened the intensity of his desire for her.

A few minutes later, and with her children in tow, Caroline tracked Abbey down to where she was gathering her things in the now-silent dressing area that had earlier buzzed with so much life and noise. 'What did you say to our Russian billionaire? Leaving, he looked like the iceberg that sank the Titanic.'

'No iceberg is that hot to trot.'

'It's not a hanging offence to fancy you, you know.' Her sister-in-law sighed. 'You are single and very attractive.'

'I didn't like him at all.' Abbey chewed anxiously at the soft underside of her lower lip. 'Did he write a cheque?'

'No, he didn't give Futures a penny.'

Abbey compressed her lips in disappointment and followed her brother's wife out to the lift that would ferry them back down to the car park. She wondered if she would lie awake all night feeling guilty about the donation that hadn't materialised because she had done nothing to encourage it. Would it have killed her to spend a couple of hours with Nikolai? She drove Caroline and the children home and saw them indoors before heading back to her apartment. Drew had been a no-show. He had sent his wife only an apologetic text. Her soft, full mouth down-curving, Abbey resolved to have a quiet word with her sibling. Caroline wasn't just her brother's wife, she was also the woman that Abbey had long regarded and trusted as her closest friend.

'So what happened to you last night?' Abbey demanded of her brother when she walked into his office the next morning. He had red hair like her and blue eyes, and was a tall man who wore metal-framed spectacles. At thirty, he was five years her senior and a qualified accountant.

'I wanted to finish the accounts before the tax man comes calling,' Drew responded. 'There's a lot of extra work to do around here since we expanded our client base. Don't forget that I have to wear two hats. I'm the firm accountant as well as your partner.'

'I know.' Abbey resisted the temptation to point out that he had been the biggest advocate for expanding the business when both she and his wife had been content with the status quo. 'Perhaps we should take on someone to help you with the accounts—'

'*No!*' Her brother disagreed with a vehemence that made her look at him in astonishment. 'Sorry, but I have my own way of doing things,' he added tautly when he intercepted her questioning glance.

'Fine.' But Abbey studied him, wondering why he was so determined not to accept help when he was obviously finding the financial side a burden. Not for the first time she wished she had a better head for juggling figures. 'I just feel that you should have had the time to come to the fashion show—'

'I'm not into fund-raising and stuff. That's Caroline's territory. I would've been a fish out of water,' he asserted.

'Caroline's lonely,' Abbey responded gently. 'You've been working late a lot recently.'

Drew shrugged. 'Caroline and I live *and* work together,' he reminded her. 'Sometimes it feels suffocating. I'm not always here in the office working when I'm late home. Sometimes I just like to go out on my own.'

Abbey was dismayed by the tenor of that admission.

Suffocating? That was not a healthy word to describe a marital relationship. 'Is there anything wrong?'

'Why should there be?' Drew frowned with annoyance at his sister. 'Why should there be anything wrong?'

'You just seem very jumpy and defensive all of a sudden.'

'You're imagining things.'

Abbey was unconvinced. 'Is there anything up with the business?'

'I'd soon tell you if there was. We could do with some more customers—'

'You told me business was brilliant—'

'Our new fancy office premises are swallowing up more of our income than I expected,' Drew admitted ruefully.

Abbey was proud that she didn't say, 'I told you so'. She was very fond of her big brother and she could see that he was under strain. He was pale, there were bags under his eyes and his nails were badly bitten, which was always a sign to the knowledgeable that Drew was stressed. 'Is there anything I can do to help?'

'Chat up the Russian billionaire. He might throw some trade our way and he must have amazing connections.'

'Caroline has already told you about Nikolai Arlov?'

'It brought some excitement into our suburban lives, didn't it? A billionaire making a move on my little sister? It doesn't happen every day.'

Abbey compressed her lips. 'I didn't like him.'

'What mortal man could match up to Jeffrey the Saint?'

'Don't call Jeffrey that!'

'Sorry, but I was never one of the devoted fans. I always thought that Jeffrey took advantage of you. You were only a kid,' Drew said in a tone of disapproval. 'If he'd been anyone other than Dad's colleague and a judge in the making, Dad would have told him to get lost.'

'Jeffrey would never have taken advantage of me. He loved me,' Abbey argued with quiet conviction. 'Look, I'd better get down to some work.'

Caroline, who worked for Support Systems from home, had faxed Abbey her appointments for the day and Abbey devoted her first hour of work to organising a housesitter for a couple going on holiday and booking their car in for a service. She was due to meet a client to chat about the arrangements for a christening party when a knock sounded on the door and heralded the delivery of flowers. Abbey got up to whisk the card out of the glorious basket of old-fashioned white and pink roses. It was not a surprise for her to see Nikolai's name on the card, but she felt almost threatened by the fact that he included his phone number. With extreme reluctance, as she did not want to encourage him, she texted him a cool, polite thank-you for the roses.

Barely a minute later, he phoned her. 'Lunch?' His dark deep voice sent a sensitised shiver down her taut spinal cord.

'Sorry, I'm too busy.'

'What do you think I am?' he riposted.

'Are you really not going to make a donation to Futures unless I go out with you?' Abbey heard herself demand without even being aware that she was going to ask that question. It told her how much that concern had been playing on her mind, even though she had told herself that she shouldn't allow his unfair tactics to weigh on her conscience.

'I never say what I don't mean.'

Abbey grimaced at her end of the phone. 'Now I feel

like I've deliberately deprived the charity of money that they badly need. How's that supposed to make me feel?'

'Hopefully bad enough to change your mind about me and give me a chance to prove what a great guy I can be.'

'Over lunch?' Abbey's conscience was taking a beating and once again she was asking herself if she should be refusing to spend just a couple of hours of her time in his company. Certainly if self-belief was a plus, he was very confident that he could win her approval.

'Make it dinner. Are you in or out?' Nikolai prompted.

'In… What time?'

'I'll pick you up at seven-thirty.'

'My address—'

'I already have it.'

'We won't get on,' she warned him ruefully.

'I'll pledge my donation this afternoon.' With that assurance Nikolai rang off.

Abbey replaced the receiver and stared at it as if it were an unexploded bomb. She could barely credit that she had agreed to see him again and that she'd allowed his tactics of bribery and pressure to win him what he wanted.

Nikolai was buoyant. He decided that she was a very clever woman. He had been keen, but now he was considerably keener. He was convinced that Abbey Carmichael knew how to play a man to heighten his interest. He instructed Sveta to contact the charity and announce his donation, and he put Olya in pursuit of the blue evening gown that Abby had modelled at the charity fashion show.

Late that afternoon, Caroline phoned Abbey in a flood of happy excitement and informed her that Nikolai had donated half a million pounds to Futures. It was the charity's largest ever single endowment and Nikolai had even promised to consider becoming a patron for the organisation. Abbey wondered what Caroline would say if she told her how the Russian had used his wealth and the charity's desperate need for funds to persuade her into seeing him again. But, just then, confessing that truth would have been the ultimate spoiler to Caroline's rare sense of achievement.

'I'm dining with Nikolai tonight,' Abbey said instead.

'That's great news. I want to see you having a good time and enjoying the fact that you're young and single!' Caroline confided cheerfully. 'And Drew just sent me flowers. He probably got the idea from Nikolai sending them to you, but who cares what prompted the gesture?'

Abbey smiled, relieved that her brother was making an effort and that Caroline was pleased. Drew's use of the word *suffocating* with regard to his marital and working life was still troubling her. She was also wondering why she hadn't asked him where he headed when he went out while she had had the chance. On the other hand, perhaps she had interfered enough. She was hardly qualified to set herself up as a marriage guidance counsellor, she reasoned ruefully. Fate hadn't allowed Abbey and Jeffrey to even get as far as a wedding night together.

The fact that they had never had the opportunity to enjoy sexual intimacy was one of Abbey's biggest sources of regret. In that field she had no precious memories to hang on to, for Jeffrey had insisted that they should wait until they were married to make love. It embarrassed Abbey to acknowledge that she was still a virgin and it was not an admission she had ever made to anyone else. Her face could still burn at the lowering recollection that her eagerness to explore those physical mysteries with the man she loved had seemed to turn him off rather than on. In retrospect she blamed her late husband's sexual reticence on his respect for her staunchly moral father and on the fact that he had been a good deal older than his bride-to-be. She studied the photo of the blond, green-eyed man with clean-cut features on her desk: Jeffrey had been a very attractive man. It was little wonder that she had fallen so hard for him and it still amazed her that he had chosen to marry a teenage school-leaver rather than one of the more eligible career women whom he met in the course of his work as a successful barrister.

Late afternoon, several impressive boxes were delivered to Abbey with Nikolai Arlov's compliments. By the time Abbey had finished unwrapping them her desk was a sea of crumpled tissue paper. She could barely credit that he had sent her the blue gown from the show in spite of her clearly stated lack of interest. That he had also thrown in the matching shoes and jewellery shook her even more. The devil was certainly in the detail.

'The clothes have arrived,' she texted him. 'Were you denied a dress-up doll as a child?'

'I only want to undress *you*,' he replied, which sent a wave of heat travelling through her and settling between her thighs in a most disturbing way.

'There's no question of that,' she texted back, shaken by his frankness and unsure of how best to deal with it. But she did not want him to harbour expectations in that line of the evening ahead of them.

She left the office earlier than was her wont and made her way home to the ultra-modern apartment where she lived. It had originally belonged to Jeffrey and the minimalist design and elegant brown and beige décor owed more to his taste than hers. Nothing she bought ever seemed to fit the sparse interior and trinkets always seemed to take on the aspect of messy clutter. Her doll's house, which was in the style of a mock stone castle, was perched on the mirrored hall table, where its fairy-tale lines looked least obtrusive. The world of minia-tures was her only hobby and the house and its miniature family of inhabitants provided a wonderful outlet for her lively imagination.

Stowing the boxes she planned to return to Nikolai, Abbey leafed through her wardrobe, instinctively searching for something as different from the blue gown as she could find. She was no man's dress-up doll! If he had an erotic fantasy she wasn't fulfilling it! She pulled out a scarlet halter-necked knee-length dress that she had bought when she was shopping with Caroline and worn only once at the staff Christmas party. After a quick shower she put on a little light make-up, teased her mane of curls into subjection and got ready. She frowned at the way the thin fabric seemed to cling all too revealingly to the full globes of her breasts and would have changed had not the doorbell buzzed.

Grabbing the boxes and her bag, she headed to the front door. A uniformed chauffeur greeted her and she handed him the boxes, accompanying him down in the lift while studying her reflection in the mirrored half-walls with dissatisfaction. The colour in her cheeks and the sparkle in her eyes implied an excitement that affronted her pride. She was, after all, only dining with Nikolai because Futures would benefit richly from her doing so. The chauffeur put the boxes in the boot of the long gleaming silver limousine and opened the passen-ger door for her.

Abbey was startled to see that Nikolai was in the car waiting for her.

'You're not wearing the dress,' he commented straight off. 'But you look almost as beautiful in red.'

Almost? Abbey was infuriated when she experienced a womanly stab of regret at not having worn the blue gown after all. 'I don't let anyone buy me clothes. I'm giving them back to you—'

'I refuse to argue with you.' Brilliant dark eyes intent, Nikolai surveyed her with raw masculine appreciation. He would not have been surprised had she shown up in jeans. She had a quirky, stroppy edge that he recognised as a challenge. This was not a woman willing to be told what to do. Mentally they were a match made in hell, he acknowledged, for she was as stubborn, individual and confrontational as he was. But at that moment he was less interested in her mind than in her body and his attention dropped to the tantalisingly ripe curve of her wine red tinted lips and the even more inviting lushness of her glorious breasts. 'I haven't stopped thinking about you for five minutes since I first saw you, *lubimaya*,' he confessed in a husky undertone.

Flattered by that assurance, Abbey was shaken once again by how strong her reaction was to him. He looked absolutely gorgeous in a silver-grey pinstripe shirt and casual jacket that was superbly tailored to his broad shoulders and powerful chest. The atmosphere between them crackled with tension. Her mouth was dry and her pulses were drumming crazily. Wildly exhilarating feelings that had nothing to do with reason were pounding through her. She focused on his lean, hard-boned face with a fascination she had never felt in her life before and she was shattered by that truth, her lashes dipping to conceal her bemused eyes and break that moment.

'What's wrong?' Quick as a flash Nikolai spoke up when she deliberately broke that visual connection with him.

Guilt was engulfing Abbey because her powerful response to Nikolai made her feel cheap and tarty, surpassing as it did anything she had ever felt for Jeffrey, whom she had fallen for at a much more innocent age. Then, she recognised that what she was feeling now was lust, pure, unvarnished lust, prompted by the sensual side of her nature, which she had had little opportunity to explore.

'Nothing's wrong,' she said flatly, fighting not to notice that his eyelashes were spiky black fringed enhancements to his beautiful eyes, that his luxuriant black hair made her fingers tingle with a sense of deprivation, that his hard male mouth filled her with curiosity and shameless longing.

'The pull between us is amazingly strong,' Nikolai remarked with an earthy smile that had an amount of charisma that took her equally by surprise. His hand closed over hers, warm and firm as if he somehow sensed her sudden urge to back away and impose some space between them. 'You have a tiny pulse beating just here...' A long brown finger brushed the fine skin above her delicate collarbone.

That glancing casual touch made Abbey shiver as if she were in a violent gale. He pulled her to him and she didn't resist. To stay upright she had to brace a hand on a lean, powerful masculine thigh. His muscles flexed beneath her touch and his dark head swooped, his mouth descending to claim hers with a fierce sexual urgency that devastated her. Her fingers smoothed over his cheekbones, delighting in the abrasive feel of his slight masculine stubble, clutched at his hair, loving the silky density of the strands, finally settling on his strong shoulders and closing there. She was struggling to stay steady in a world that was shot through with multi-coloured fireworks of excitement and sensation. Her body was responding like a parched plant to life-giving water. She loved the taste and feel of him and couldn't get enough of either. The erotic plunge of his tongue made heat and moisture surge between her thighs and stirred an ache there that was so intense it almost hurt. He had awakened a need she had ignored for too long and she pushed against him, hungrily reaching out and greedy for every sensation she could grab.

He undid the halter of her dress and the bra beneath before she could even guess what he was about and took immediate advantage of his access to her sensitive flesh. His hands cupped the weight of her voluptuous breasts and he buried his mouth with an appreciative murmur against a fragrant freckled creamy slope while the pads of his fingers skilfully chafed the swollen jut of her nipples.

'You are the most amazingly sexy woman,' he breathed thickly.

It was not how Abbey saw herself and the comment stunned her back into possession of her senses. Suddenly she felt naked and exposed and foolish. She reached down and yanked her clothing back up over her bare skin, struggling with clumsy hands to retie the straps. He dragged her hands out of the way and performed the task for her.

'I don't do stuff like this,' she muttered as if she was

excusing herself, but her eager body refused to resist when he tugged her back into his arms.

'This is different. We're different. I've never been so hot for anyone as I am for you, *milaya*.' Long fingers delving into her mass of rippling red curls, Nikolai muttered something else in Russian and pressed her hand against his aching groin with an explicit need that shocked and excited her in equal degrees. That bold invitation fascinated her. With a thrill of awareness she felt the hard thrusting power and shape of his boldly aroused manhood beneath the barrier of his trousers. Light-headed with the strength of her desire, she moaned beneath the marauding ravishment of his hot mouth, her fingers sliding between his shirt and his belt to explore the taut hair-roughened skin of his flat, muscular stomach and trace the aggressive length of his erection. He groaned beneath her inexpert ministrations and that open responsiveness and unashamed hunger of his allowed her to glory in her feminine power for the first time in her life. She felt drunk on the daring of what she was doing.

'I want you now...I don't want to wait,' Nikolai growled thickly.

That uncharacteristic sense of daring that had momentarily fired Abbey shrivelled and died. She whipped her hand away from him, shattered by her total loss of control. 'This is wrong...this is not me. I hardly know you.'

'You know everything that matters,' Nikolai told her harshly as the limousine came to a halt.

Abbey glanced out in confusion at the apartment building in one of London's most exclusive residential areas. 'Where are we?'

'My home.'

'I assumed we'd be dining out some place,' Abbey

remarked uncomfortably as the passenger door beside her opened.

'The paparazzi give me no peace in public places.'

Abbey knew that had to be true. Press interest in his movements, most particularly his love-life, was considerable and she had no wish to see her own name in print next to his. His minders urged her protectively towards the steps and the door already opening for their entrance.

'Will you need me again this evening, sir?' his chauffeur enquired.

'No. I'll see you in the morning,' Nikolai responded easily.

Colour flushing her cheeks and dismay and annoyance flaring within at that revealing instruction, Abbey breathed in slow and deep and smoothed down her frock before crossing the elegant foyer to board the waiting lift.

'Could I have a word with you?' Abbey asked Nikolai in a civil tone as she passed by the middle-aged manservant on the doorstep of his penthouse apartment.

A moment later, she was in a spectacular high-ceilinged reception room decorated in opulent shades of cream and gold and furnished with polished antiques. Nikolai closed the door and quirked a questioning black brow. 'What's the problem?'

'The problem? I heard what you said to your driver when you told him you wouldn't need him again this evening. I'm not sleeping with you tonight and how dare you assume that I will!'

Nikolai dealt her a frowning appraisal.

'You're not about to persuade me otherwise, so

don't waste your time trying!' Abbey continued furiously, her temper rising at the uneasy suspicion that her conduct in the limo had given him every reason to hope that she might well share his bed without any further ado…

CHAPTER THREE

CHAPTER THREE

'I WASN'T aware that I had been guilty of making any
assumption, so your attack is somewhat premature and
excessive,' Nikolai imparted very drily.

Abbey stabbed the air between them with an em-
phatic finger. 'I agreed to dine with you this evening—
that's *all!* Perhaps you feel that you're entitled to more
for a charitable donation of half a million, but my body
was never on the table...'

Steady dark eyes rested on her. 'The table would be
a little hard on both of us,' he murmured with sardonic
amusement. 'Where did you get the impression that I
have to buy women into my bed?'

'You held your donation to Futures over my head!'
Abbey condemned hotly. 'You told me that you would
use any angle to get what you want, didn't you?'

'But I don't pay for sex,' Nikolai spelt out cool as ice.
'I don't *ever* under any circumstances *pay* for sex.'

Abbey lost colour, her freckles standing out against
her pallor. His conviction washed over her like a bucket
of chilling water, dousing her anger and leaving her uncertain of her position. 'What about the dress, the shoes
and the jewellery?'

'I'm a generous guy. The women I meet enjoy and expect that sort of gesture from me.'

'You meet the wrong kind of women.'

'Perhaps. But it is offensive to suggest that I need to use my money to persuade a woman into my bed.'

'Let's not get bogged down in the irrelevant!' Abbey broke in. 'I heard you dismiss your driver for the evening.'

'Perhaps I was planning to drive you home later myself,' Nikolai murmured silkily, although the faintest tinge of dark colour demarcated his high cheekbones, for her assumption about his expectations had been one-hundred-per-cent accurate. He *had* assumed that she would share his bed that night. Her absolute lack of sophistication and tact on that score amazed him. He had never in his life endured such a clumsy scene with a woman. But then, sex had never, ever been something withheld or denied to him. His healthy libido was unaccustomed to the practice of patience. He thought that she was remarkably naïve for a married woman who might have been expected to know how to handle sexual matters a little more smoothly and without this odd undertone of prudish hysteria.

Abbey went pink at that easy explanation, which should have occurred to her as a possibility but which for some reason had not. 'It's just...I hardly know you...'

Nikolai was amused by her embarrassment. Suddenly she seemed much younger than her twenty-five years and almost as awkward as a leggy schoolgirl. His stunning dark eyes unusually warm with amusement and his annoyance evaporating fast, he extended a shapely brown hand. 'Let's eat, *milaya*,' he suggested.

After tonight, Abbey promised herself that she would never see him again. She didn't like what he made her feel. She still recalled her first glimpse of Jeffrey at the age of fifteen. Her father had brought him home for dinner one evening and she had been so mesmerised by Jeffrey's classic blond good looks that she had barely eaten a mouthful. In retrospect she was ashamed of herself—how superficial she had been in those days! That same year Drew had got engaged to Caroline and set a wedding date, so Jeffrey and his parents had become a regular feature at family events.

Abbey had fallen head over heels for the handsome barrister in her father's chambers, impressed as much by Jeffrey's keen intelligence and the rumour that his success and reputation in court had already ensured that he was earmarked to become a judge. She had been content to love him from afar and console herself with occasional brief conversations. He had never seemed anything more than polite and pleasant to her until the day he asked her out to dinner, surprising her with that invitation as much as his move seemed to surprise everyone else in their respective families. How many weeks had it been before Jeffrey even kissed her goodnight? There could be no comparison between the two men: Jeffrey, who had genuinely loved and respected her, and Nikolai Danilovich Arlov to whom she was simply another potential sexual conquest. How could she have responded to such a man? Where were her pride and self-respect?

'What are you thinking about?' Nikolai prompted in the imposing dining room as the first course was delivered, for the faraway look in her face was unmistakable.

Abbey reddened and ducked her bright head and rubbed nervously at her wedding ring with the pad of her thumb. 'Nothing important.'

But Nikolai had noted that revealing contact with the gold ring on her finger and was convinced otherwise. He sensed that he was in competition with her memories of the very special man she had mentioned. The suspicion that her mind wandered to her dead husband even when she was in Nikolai's company infuriated him. It was the very first time that he could remember considering or even caring about what a woman might be thinking about when she was with him.

'What age were you when you got married?'

Abbey gave him a surprised look. 'Nineteen.'

'That's very young.'

'I was old enough to know what I was doing.'

'What age was your husband?'

Abbey tensed, reluctant to answer that question. 'Thirty-nine.'

Nikolai dealt her an incredulous look. 'He was old enough to be your father!'

'You're being very rude,' Abbey told him curtly. 'Jeffrey was handsome, successful and very much in demand socially. I think very few women would have regarded him in that light.'

Nikolai shrugged, well aware that some men went for very much younger women. He was only thirty-three years old, but the idea of bedding a giggly teenager with no experience of men or the world repulsed him. He could only think that Jeffrey Carmichael must have been inadequate in some way to choose such an unequal partner as a wife.

'How long have you been a widow?' he queried.

'Six years—'

'So you couldn't have been married that long.'

Abbey realised that he didn't know as much about her

as she had assumed. She told him about the sixteen-year-old drunken joyrider who had caused the accident as the wedding party travelled between church and reception.

Nikolai was sincerely shocked by the story. 'That was tragic—particularly when your sister-in-law was seriously injured as well.'

'It ripped the heart out of two families. Jeffrey's parents have both passed away since then and are sadly missed.'

'And you're still mourning?' Nikolai prompted.

Abbey nodded confirmation. 'You don't forget a love like that.'

'But you and your husband were together such a short time.'

'Time's immaterial.'

'Yet you won't stay with me tonight, even though it's what we both want?'

A hot rush of pink discomfiture mantling her cheeks, Abbey decided that it would be undignified arguing that point and she began to eat instead. 'That's different.'

Nikolai stroked the back of her clenched hand with a mocking fingertip. 'I know. I'm not asking you to love me.'

Abbey suppressed a shiver of reaction as she recalled the hot hunger of his mouth on hers and the desire he had unleashed inside her. 'I don't need the warning.'

Nikolai surveyed her in frustration. 'So you've already made up your mind about me?'

'That we don't suit? Yes,' Abbey admitted.

'But we share an amazing passion.'

'That's not important to me.'

'It is to me.'

'But by next week you'll find it with someone else,' Abbey told him with a calm insouciance that set his even white teeth on edge.

'If I thought that I wouldn't have gone to so much trouble to persuade you to come here.'

Nikolai made a rare effort to be entertaining by finding out what interested her. He was on his very best behaviour. Checking her watch over the coffee, Abbey was taken aback when she realised just how much time had passed over the delicious meal. He was highly intelligent and excellent company and she was dismayed by how much she had contrived to enjoy herself.

'I don't want to be too late tonight because I have an early start in the morning.'

As she rose from behind the table Nikolai followed suit. He pulled her to him with confident hands. 'You could have an early start with me.'

As she thought of it a tremor ran through her, sexual heat curling low in her pelvis. Desire was in her now like a dark enemy, undermining her defences. She had a dim picture of him lying on tumbled white sheets. She remembered how she had lost her head with him in the limo and knew that he would be utterly irresistible in less inhibiting circumstances. He bent his handsome dark head and took her parted lips with devouring hunger. She quivered against him, her heart racing as fast as the blood in her veins, driven by a heady combination of excitement and longing. Disturbed by the intensity of what she was feeling, she stiffened.

'I'm going home,' she breathed when he lifted his head again.

Paparazzi were waiting outside the building when they emerged. Cameras went off even as Nikolai's security team made the waiting photographers back off and give them a clear passage to the glossy black Ferrari now parked in readiness by the kerb. Her colour high as demands for her name were loudly shot at her, Abbey climbed into the car with her head down, reluctant to give anyone the chance to get a decent picture of her.

'They'll follow us back to your apartment so that they can identify you,' Nikolai forecast.

'Surely not?' But even as she spoke she saw two men jumping onto motorbikes across the road and her heart sank. 'Is it always like this for you?'

'I hate it,' he breathed. 'By tomorrow morning at least one paper will have offered you cash to talk about me.'

'I won't do it. Your secrets are safe with me. The colour of your dining-room wallpaper will go to the grave with me,' she promised him.

He burst out laughing at that sally.

They were tailed all the way back to her apartment block and she didn't object when he insisted on seeing her indoors, because even before she climbed out of his car she saw several men race across the pavement to lie in wait for them again. But when one of them aimed a camera, Nikolai's minders stepped in and snatched it away. An altercation broke out between the men as Nikolai urged her through the entrance to the building with a protective arm splayed to her narrow spine.

'You don't need to come all the way upstairs,' she said as the lift doors sprang open beside them.

An ebony brow climbed. 'I won't overstay my welcome,' he declared.

He took the key out of her fingers and pressed open the front door to follow her in. 'A model castle,' he said in surprise, crossing the hall to peer into it.

'It's a doll's house. I always wanted one when I was a child but I had to wait until I grew up and could afford to buy my own.'

A moment's appraisal of his surroundings had been sufficient to assure Nikolai of the modern minimalist nature of her home, so the interior of the fairy-tale castle was a revelation. A red-headed miniature doll in a voluminous white lace nightdress was getting ready to climb into a curtained four-poster bed. Two tiny Siamese cats were curled up by the blazing fire. Every inch of doll's house space was packed with diminutive antique furniture and every surface was cluttered with books, art and bric-a-brac. Although a little row of beds and a cot in the attic occupied by several weeny dolls testified to the existence of a large family of children, there wasn't a man in the whole building. He wondered if she appreciated how much that cosy domestic fantasy revealed of her true nature.

'Interesting,' he remarked truthfully.

Abbey hovered. She wanted him to kiss her again and despised herself for her weakness. She could no more have walked away and denied that temptation than she could have stopped breathing. The tip of her tongue slid out to moisten her full lower lip. She saw his attention drop to her mouth and linger and she tried the tongue trick again. Even as she did it quite deliberately to attract, she was shocked and incredulous at the way she was behaving. He groaned something in his own language and hauled her to him, a long-fingered hand splaying across the swell of her bottom to gather her close. The expert dart of his tongue into the moist cavern between her lips set her on fire as much as the unmistakable hard male heat of his erection. She shivered violently against his lean muscular physique, her knees trembling under her. It had never occurred to her that wanting might hurt so much or that she might be quite so hungry for a man's passion.

Nikolai scored the pad of his finger along the swollen curve of her lush lower lip in wonderment: he couldn't believe she was sending him away unsatisfied. Her pupils were dilated, her breathing as fractured as his own. She was as hot for him as he was for her. 'You burn me up,' he confided. 'When can I see you again?'

'This was a one-off,' Abbey reminded him uncomfortably.

'You can't be serious.'

Abbey stiffened and pulled back from him, imposing the physical separation that her every sense and urge protested. 'I'm afraid that I am.'

Smouldering dark golden eyes assailed her evasive gaze. 'Let me stay...'

'No.' Her breath snarled up in her dry throat while her imagination took erotic wing. She envisaged her body entwined in intimacy with the lean hard potency of his and her tummy contracted, tiny burning sensations stabbing low in her pelvis. All of a sudden she was a woman she didn't know and couldn't comprehend. Self-control had never been a problem for her and, aside of her understandable regrets over her unconsummated marriage, she had never dreamt that sex might be so important to her. But now, while she trembled in a man's presence with the heat and damp of arousal blossoming between her legs, the extent of her own ignorance terrified her. Nikolai was tearing her inside out with sexual longing and that truth made her cringe.

He brought up his hands and used them to frame her stunning violet eyes as he gazed down at her with brooding frustration. 'I won't leave you alone—'

'You *must*,' she told him. 'I don't believe in casual sex.'

'And that's all that I will offer, *lubimaya*. I don't have anything else to give.'

'And what's your excuse?'

'*Excuse?*' His smooth ebony brows drew together in a frown of incomprehension.

'I don't do casual sex because I believe in love and commitment.'

'I only commit to sex.' Only inches away from her, Nikolai tilted her back up against him. 'And I'm very good at it.'

All of a quiver, eyes starry, cheeks pink, she stared up at him, mesmerised by a sexual charisma and presence that left her brain as befuddled as a magic spell. He kissed her again, slowly, savouring every nuance of her helpless response. His forefingers curled into the hem of her dress and trailed back up her slim thighs, lifting the fabric out of his path.

'No, Nikolai,' Abbey breathed, shaking from the gliding brush of his skilful fingers against her slender thighs, her mind leaping ahead of his every move to picture an even more exciting development.

'*Da, Nikolai*, is what I want and need to hear,' he murmured thickly, toying with and teasing her mouth with his lips and the edge of his even white teeth. '*Ti takaya nezhnaya.*'

'What does it mean?'

'You are so beautiful. I don't want to tear myself away to go home.'

For an insane moment she considered telling him that he could stay if he promised not to touch her. She didn't want him to leave. She didn't want to be alone either. The idea of lying in a man's arms was hugely appealing. The idea of waking up with company for a change was even more seductive. She was dismayed by her own naïvety, flinching from the raw amusement she would rouse with such a silly proposition. He wanted sex. He wanted to treat her like her many predecessors in his bed—women he had enjoyed for a few weeks without love or strings of any kind before moving on to the next. Could she really want to join that nameless herd? Someone whom he used to satisfy his lust for a night or two before he became bored and sought the fresh stimulation of a new face and body?

CHAPTER FOUR

'I LOVE your hair,' Nikolai continued softly, combing long, lean fingers gently through the heavy fall of curls that were the colour of maple leaves in autumn, 'and the softness of your skin.' Having exposed the smooth silky flesh where Abbey's slender neck met her shoulder, he buried his lips there.

The erotic touch of his mouth in that precise spot was like an electric charge to Abbey's senses. It made her unbearably aware of the tight, pulsing sensitivity of her nipples and the hollow ache between her thighs. Both sensations urged her closer to the masculine promise of his hard physique, her breathing audible, her body on fire with a frustration that she was only just beginning to recognise. It was an ungovernable hunger that was flooding through her like an unleashed dam and threatening to wash away her every inhibition. She would never have believed until that moment how powerful such promptings could be. She would never have credited that the fierce sensual pressure of a man's mouth and the probing invasion of his tongue could make her shake as if she were an accident victim.

'Nikolai...' Abbey whispered, shocked by the force of what she was feeling and frightened by it.

His lean strong face tightened at the recognisable plea in her voice. Though she was eager to deny it, she wanted him as much as he wanted her. Fierce satisfaction gripped him until he noticed the photo of the bridal couple on the wall behind her. It was Abbey in full bridal regalia and her late husband—a handsome, smirking blond guy. Inexplicably Nikolai's level of satisfaction sank. He reminded himself that he didn't go for demanding women. As far as possible he kept his sex life straightforward and simple. There was nothing either straightforward or simple about the beautiful outspoken redhead in front of him. There was nothing either simple or straightforward about what he was thinking either: had she once wanted the blond guy as much as she now wanted him? That struck Nikolai as a deeply freaky thought and he could not imagine why his mind had come up with such a strange reflection, for why should he want to compete with a dead man?

Abbey was way beyond thinking, she could only feel, and when Nikolai drew back from her she felt fiercely deprived and lonely. She wrapped her arms round his shoulders to bring him back to her, her mouth as hungry for his as for an invigorating elixir. Her fingertips flirted with the luxuriant black strands at the back of his well-shaped head. Touching him, she discovered, was an addictive pleasure. Her breasts swelled in connection with the hard muscular wall of his chest and the sting of her nipples eased beneath that welcome pressure. Her body sang at every point of contact with his. A lean hand closed over a full pouting breast and it felt as if her whole body lit up in eager response. A dulled moan escaped her as he moulded her tender flesh, the pads of his thumbs finding the erect points of sensitivity with devastating accuracy. Each kiss filled her with desperate craving for the next. Passion had erupted in her like an oil gusher and it was too new and too seductive to be capped and denied. Every dart of his tongue released another intoxicating surge of sensation.

The exact moment when he pushed her skirt higher was known to her, not because panic or denial assailed her, but because her impatience was greater than his and she was already desperate for him to touch her with greater intimacy. An exploring masculine fingertip skated over the fabric of her boxer-cut knickers and discovered the moist heat at the heart of her. Her breath caught in her throat and she gasped as he skated that caress up over her prominent mound where every nerve-ending leapt in an agony of sweet sensation. He kept his attention there and her legs shook with the stress of having to stay upright. She clung to his broad shoulders and pushed against him. With a groan he hauled her bodily up into his arms.

'Where's your bed?' he growled against her satin-smooth cheek and paused for an instant to investigate the delicate expanse below her small ear, the intrinsic scent of her skin acting like an aphrodisiac on him.

Abbey was weightless with desire and longing. She couldn't find her voice: she indicated the door at the other end of the hall and he took her there to what had once been Jeffrey's bed, which she had never shared with her late husband or any other man. And she remembered that and inwardly cringed and hated herself; yet she could no more have pushed Nikolai away and denied herself than she could have wilfully stopped breathing. Nikolai shed his shoes, his socks and his jacket and came down on the bed with her. Abbey yanked him free of his tie and began to unbutton his shirt. In some corner of her mind she could not credit that it was she who was doing such things. But as she tugged his shirt free of the waistband of his trousers and the edges parted to display a hair-roughened bronzed slice of powerful chest her pleasure in the sight wiped out her self-doubt. His brilliant eyes were bright in his lean dark face and she was utterly entrapped by the impact of them, her heart banging as if she were running a marathon race.

Nikolai undid the ties on the halter-neck dress and bra and released a masculine groan of satisfaction when the lush abundance of her creamy curves spilled free of the constraining fabric once again. He lowered his head to the rigid pink peaks that crowned them and whisked her nipples with his tongue while his hands shaped the soft, silken swell of the pouting mounds.

Besieged by tormenting sensation, Abbey moaned out loud, her fingers sinking into his tousled black hair to pull him back to her. They shared a passionate kiss before the allure of her breasts tempted him back there, while at the same time he extracted her from the dress caught round her hips.

'I've never felt like this before,' Nikolai breathed in an unguarded admission that took even him by surprise.

Abbey parted her lips to match his confession, but then fell silent at the recollection of Jeffrey, which threatened a comparison too tasteless and painful to be endured. Nikolai searched her smoky violet eyes and sensed her reticence and its cause and it annoyed the hell out of him at that moment. He was offended by the conviction that he was continually having to measure up to another man in her estimation.

Nikolai crushed her swollen lips beneath his again, darting and delving his tongue until she responded with matching fervour. He peeled off her last garment with alacrity, surveying the voluptuous violin curves of her lush body with intense pleasure. 'You have the most glorious shape, *milaya moya*.'

The madness that had seized Abbey thinned like a cloud of fog and she marvelled that she could be lying naked for this man's admiration. But, in truth, she found his unconcealed reverence and appreciation for her body absolutely thrilling. For the first time in her life she felt sexy and feminine and proud of her curvaceous figure. But shyness and insecurity still threatened to break through the ache of arousal that held her taut and imprisoned by his spell.

Nikolai trailed a skilful hand along a slender thigh to the tenderest place of all and the last fetters of control fell from her. He probed the tight, wet depths of her secret centre and she was lost beyond reclaim in sensation and response. He caressed the tiny bud beneath the auburn curls with the pad of his thumb and instant sensation exploded inside her, sending an earthquake of desire cascading through her in a liquid surge.

'Please...' she mumbled, barely knowing what she was saying or even asking for.

Nikolai dug contraception out of his wallet one-handed. He gazed down at her, stunned by the response she was giving him. She was so lovely with her coppery hair spread across the pillow, her delicate face flushed with soft colour, her blue eyes half closed with passion. For a split second he hesitated, for he suspected that afterwards she might have regrets, for it was a challenge for him to believe that she had changed her mind about him so totally. But rampant arousal and need powered Nikolai. He wanted her with a hunger stronger than anything he had ever felt before and self-denial of any kind was not in his genes.

'*Ti nuzhna mne*—I need you,' he asserted in a roughened undertone.

His lean, darkly handsome face was taut with desire and his stunning eyes were locked to her in a look that made her feel a million dollars. Jeffrey had never seemed to need her or look at her in such a way. Even as her brain recoiled from that treacherous thought her spine arched with the spellbinding excitement of Nikolai's lovemaking. Her heart was thundering, her entire body quivering with the strain.

He spread her under him and paused only to don protection before tilting her up to him and driving into her with a single powerful thrust. She was incredibly tight and he came to a halt, moving with greater caution and concern. 'But you were married,' he exclaimed when she cried out.

For a moment she had recoiled in surprise from the sharp pain of his entrance. Only then did she appreciate why it had hurt and why he was bewildered. 'It was never consummated,' she told him grudgingly.

Nikolai studied her in frank wonderment. 'Even before the wedding? You mean you never once had sex...? That's crazy.'

In the heat of the passion that had brought her to bed with a man she barely knew it seemed crazy to Abbey as well. But she understood that she wasn't thinking straight just then. Even as her mind was clearing her body was quickening with renewed excitement as Nikolai sank into her again and the delicious friction of his movements sent a wave of irresistible pleasure coursing through her.

'Oh...' she moaned, her body rising to meld with his in helpless response.

Nikolai was making a real effort to be gentle, which was a new departure for him. He was stunned by the awareness that he was her first lover and eager to match whatever expectations she might have of him.

'Don't stop,' Abbey urged, frustrated by the feeling that she was reaching for some ultimate reaction that was still being denied her.

'You feel like satin and velvet. I don't *ever* want to stop,' Nikolai growled, ravishing her with long, skilled strokes.

The exquisite pleasure rose to a delirious tormenting peak that made Abbey writhe beneath him. Her whole being was engulfed by the driving need to satisfy the ache he had evoked. Her heart pounding, she surrendered to the erotic pulsing heat of his driving body. When the unbearable tension and excitement gave way to an ecstatic shuddering convulsion of extreme pleasure, she screamed. Afterwards she fell into a cocoon of sweet drowning satiation, her limbs weighted to the bed by exhaustion.

But her mind was in no way able to practise the same inaction. Nikolai achieved the same pleasure with a shuddering growl and she snaked away from him in the same instant, rejection and distaste assailing her in a powerful wave. She could not believe what she had done. The horror of having slept with Nikolai Arlov held her fast even as the last tiny tremors of sexual satisfaction rippled through her. Not only had she betrayed everything she had ever believed in, she had betrayed the pure, precious love she had shared with Jeffrey. And she was genuinely appalled.

Thrust away from the embrace of her warm female body at the ultimate wrong moment, Nikolai attempted to urge her back to him. 'Come here, *lubimaya*.'

Abbey viewed him with hostile smoky blue eyes. 'Don't touch me!' she yelled at him in immediate rejection of his touch. Pushing him away, she scrambled off the bed at speed to snatch up the dressing gown lying on a nearby chair and envelop her slim body in its folds.

Nikolai sat up. Rage was roaring through him like a bushfire. The violence of her rejection stung like an acid bath stripping his skin from his bones. 'I assume this is a case of remorse *after* the event.'

Abbey was trembling with distress. She flung him a furious glance. 'What else? I'd like you to leave now.'

'Isn't it a little late for that? We have just made love,' Nikolai reminded her drily.

'And it was the biggest mistake I've ever made!' Abbey launched at him wrathfully.

'No, it was a normal, natural event for a passionate woman,' Nikolai contradicted levelly. 'It's not a sin to want or enjoy sex.'

Abbey was outraged that he had the nerve to stick around and argue with her and, worst of all, throw her enjoyment back in her teeth. She wanted him gone. She wanted to shower, change the bedding, eradicate every piece of evidence that he had ever been in her apartment, never mind her bed. She hated him, but she hated herself even more.

'I was weak and you took advantage of that. Well, what else could I expect from a guy like you? A guy who knows the price of everything and the value of nothing!'

Nikolai sprang upright, six feet three inches of lean, bronzed, magnificent nudity and an arresting sight in her prettily decorated pastel bedroom. 'How dare you speak to me like this? You invited me into your bed. You wanted me…'

Abbey could not bear that reminder. Her face burning with embarrassment and remorse, she stared at Jeffrey's photo by the bed and her sense of shame almost choked her. 'I'll never forgive myself for wanting you and betraying everything I believe in.'

Nikolai had already had more than enough without having that assurance hurled at him. He pulled on his boxers and gathered up the rest of his clothes without ceremony before striding out of the room and across the hall to the bathroom. He had never been so offended. His anger was like a big black stone inside him, weighing him down. It had not occurred to him that she might be a drama queen with no manners. It had certainly not occurred to him that he might have the best sex of a lifetime with such a woman. A virgin as eager for him as he had been for her, who had decided to be ashamed of what they had shared rather than proud of it. It was not a female reaction that had ever come his way before. Worse still, he had only to summon her face into his mind to feel his body surge and harden with fierce hunger for her again.

Remorse attacked Abbey while he was gone. She had responded to his advances and slept with him. Her regrets were not his fault, but, although intellectually she accepted that, she also sensed that Nikolai was intelligent enough to have known how she would feel and yet he had still taken what was on offer. She was in the bedroom doorway when he reappeared.

'I know you don't understand how I feel,' she breathed tautly. 'But I once loved and was loved by someone very special and, tonight, I feel I betrayed that bond with an intimacy that was meaningless and empty.'

Although Nikolai had never sought meaning in sex, he was more insulted than ever by a declaration that once again demoted him to second-rate status and he sent her a sardonic appraisal. 'Your husband has been dead for six years. You should have moved on by now.'

'It's not that easy.'

'And your deifying the dead won't make the process any easier,' Nikolai told her drily.

'I don't think you've ever loved anyone.'

Nikolai thought about that. 'No woman. I loved my grandfather,' he admitted in a rare burst of confidence, 'but your grief strikes me as obsessive.'

'That's my business,' Abbey told him defensively.

'As you say.' Nikolai opened the door. '*Dubroynochi*, goodnight,' he drawled softly before he pulled the door closed behind him.

Abbey wrapped her arms round herself in the silent hall and snatched in a charged breath. She was still in shock. Indeed her entire body was quivering uncomfortably in the aftermath of the passion they had shared. A passion such as she had never dreamt existed, and her body ached from it. She wondered why she felt so much more alone than usual and what it was about Nikolai that got to her to such an extent. She found him amazingly attractive and that was incredibly hard to cope with. Jeffrey had never desired her to that extent. It was a disloyal thought and even thinking it bothered her, but Abbey believed in being honest with herself. Jeffrey might have loved her enough to make her his wife, but when it came to the physical side of their relationship he had been more lukewarm than passionate. Perhaps she had been the more highly sexed of the two of them, she reasoned frantically, but her sense of guilt simply deepened. She barely slept a wink that night.

The next morning she received a phone call from a well-known tabloid offering her money to talk about her date with Nikolai. She turned it down with disdain. It was an unpleasant surprise to be greeted by a crowd of paparazzi and cameras when she drove out of the underground car park to head to work. Her face was hot enough to fry eggs on while she wondered if the journalists appreciated that Nikolai had got her into bed on the first date, fully living up to his notorious reputation with women.

When she arrived at Support Systems, two rather grim-looking men were striding out of the building. 'Who were those men just leaving?' Abbey asked, walking into her brother's office.

Drew was pale and he shot her a troubled glance. 'Potential customers. I didn't like the look of them, so we won't be taking them on.'

'They looked like bouncers.'

'Oddly enough, that's pretty much what they are. They wanted us to hire more security staff for a West End club—not our field of expertise, I explained.'

'No, indeed, but then we do say in our literature that we'll have a go at any task that the customer needs done,' Abbey pointed out.

Her brother frowned. 'We have to draw the line somewhere. By the way, you have an appointment in an hour with Nikolai Arlov—'

'*Nikolai?* What does he want?' Abbey gasped in dismay.

'I haven't a clue, but hopefully he wants to put some lucrative work our way. Why are you so shocked? I understand that you dined with him last night.'

'Yes.' But Abbey was outraged by the idea that Nikolai still had the nerve to try to make her do what she didn't want to do. He had to be well aware that she never wanted to see him again in this lifetime, so why set up an appointment with her? Last night she had dined with him purely because of his donation to Futures. Too late had she recognised the trap she had fallen into in allowing him to effectively buy her indulgence and her time. That had given him entirely the wrong message. Just how had she failed to appreciate what a ruthless bastard she was dealing with?

'Do we really need more work?' Abbey pressed.

'Very much so,' her brother emphasised.

Abbey went into her own office, where her assistant asked her to call back a catering firm that had been in touch about an unpaid bill. Abbey frowned, for she had assumed that the bill had been settled weeks earlier, and went to check Support Systems' bank statements. Her skin turned clammy and shock brought up goose bumps on her flesh when she saw the parade of minus signs on the first statement that warned that the company was running on a substantial overdraft. Naturally, she knew that they had an agreed overdraft facility, for occasionally clients were slow to pay, but she had not been aware of quite how tight matters were in the financial field.

Drew was irritable when she questioned him. 'It's not my fault you don't keep up with the latest bank statements,' he told her with a curtness that made her view him in surprise.

'I know, but I didn't appreciate that we were quite so short of funds. What's brought that about?'

'All our operating costs have risen and we have some very late payers on our books.'

'Give me the names,' Abbey urged, feeling guilty that she had not kept abreast of the firm's dwindling cash-flow situation. 'I'll chase them up for payment.'

As she returned to her office to make good on that proposal she thought that it would be a good idea for her to spend an evening going through the accounts in an attempt to identify exactly when and how things had gone wrong. Just a few months earlier, Support Systems had been riding high with more clients than they could cope with. Unhappily, expansion appeared to have come at a massive cost in overheads. Even so, while that overdraft might suggest a downturn in the firm's fortunes, Abbey and her colleagues were still so busy they were run off their feet.

Chasing up the firm's debtors gave her little time to agonise over the approaching interview with Nikolai. But as she crossed the city to the massive office block that housed the UK headquarters of Arlov Industries she was painfully aware that, while she might not want to accept work from Nikolai, Support Systems currently needed all the business it could get. Even so she totally hated and despised him for forcing her to face him again and in a professional capacity. He was the very last man alive she wanted to see again.

CHAPTER FIVE

WHILE Abbey waited in the elegant reception area on the top floor, she was conscious of being under scrutiny. She was already aware of the identity of two of the women who had wandered out past reception to get a better look at her: she recognised both Olya and Darya from the audience at the fashion show.

Furthermore, she, too, was human and curious and she had checked out Nikolai on the Internet before dining with him. She had marvelled at how much information there was about him that in effect gave very few actual facts. His exact background might be shrouded in mystery, but the trio of stunning Russian beauties who acted as his executive team were a modern-day business legend. Sveta, Olya and Darya were frequently referred to in suggestive terms as Nikolai's 'stable' or 'harem'. All three women were highly educated and well qualified for the positions they held in his empire, but their sheer physical beauty, and the level of trust and intimacy they enjoyed with their oligarch employer, had encouraged more provocative interpretations of their relationship with him. Several of Nikolai's past lovers had complained of having to compete with the trio for his attention.

Ten minutes after her arrival, Abbey was escorted into a large airy office in which Nikolai was working with his Russian aides. Nikolai crossed the floor to greet her. 'I appreciate your punctuality,' he told her.

She was shattered by the pure impact of his potent dark beauty on her senses. His straight ebony brows highlighted the brooding dark depth of his spectacular eyes that were enhanced by inky black lashes. The strong blade of his arrogant nose bisected high cheekbones, throwing into prominence a strong masculine jaw and a perfectly modelled wide sensual mouth. One glance at his lean, dark, dazzlingly handsome face and her mouth ran dry and her breath shortened in her throat as if an electric shock had gone through her. His natural grace of movement only added to his potent level of virile attraction by welding her attention to him. Recognising that she was being closely watched by his three female executives, Abbey experienced the sudden fear that her responses could be read on her face. In reaction to that daunting thought she felt her skin heat with self-conscious colour and she scolded herself furiously for acting like a blushing schoolgirl at an important business meeting. Her mood was not improved by a flashback of recollection from the night before that scorched colour as far as her hairline and dampened her upper lip with perspiration.

'Everything that we discuss within this room will be highly confidential,' Nikolai warned her.

'Of course,' she acceded as he introduced his aides and then dismissed them.

Abbey discovered that she was relieved to no longer be the centre of attention for three sharp pairs of female eyes.

Nikolai studied Abbey with the appraising attention

of a connoisseur. Her black trouser suit and yellow shirt
were standard business-issue apparel, but she wore them
with cool elegance. He appreciated her height and her
proud carriage almost as much as the sleek line of her
shapely curves and long, endless legs. She wore her
fabulous mane of colourful hair in a high ponytail. Tiny
coppery curls had escaped to soften her hairline and a
hint of make-up accentuated her remarkable violet eyes
and her soft full pink mouth. She looked incredibly
young and untouched for a married woman, he reflected
grimly. And, now, as the male who had discovered and
taken her innocence for himself, he knew the literal
truth of that observation.

The familiar tightening at his groin infuriated him,
for he had spent half of the previous night in a cold
shower, his hunger for her refusing to abate. It incensed
him that he should still lust after her to that extent. It
didn't make sense after the way she had treated him
either. He wanted to walk away and turn his back on her
without a thought, something he had contrived to do
with every other woman he had ever known. He didn't
want her to be different or exceptional in any way. And
he remained very curious about the kind of man who
had chosen to leave such a beauty virginally intact. In
fact he had already instructed Sveta to check out the late
Jeffrey Carmichael and bring him a detailed report.

Abbey gritted her teeth in the heavy silence. 'After
the way we parted, I'm sure you can understand my
surprise when I got to the office this morning and discovered that you had made an appointment to see me.'

'I want you to work for me—'

'Work for you? After last night? Are you out of your
mind?' Abbey demanded thinly, dragging her straying

attention from his fabulous bone structure and scolding herself for looking at him in the first place.

'Not at all.'

'I refuse to work for you in any capacity!' Her violet eyes flashed a warning to him, her slender figure rigid with animosity.

'At least hear me out first,' Nikolai drawled, his gaze lingering on the ripple of her shirt as she breathed in and the way the fine silky fabric clung and outlined her wonderfully lush curves. 'But I should also make it clear that I won't accept you delegating the responsibility of working for me either to your employees or to other professionals whom you may choose to engage on my behalf.'

In receipt of that comprehensive embargo, which would make personal contact with him unavoidable, Abbey focused on him with angry incredulous intensity. Noticing where his unrepentant gaze was resting, she began buttoning her jacket with scarlet cheeks and hands that were trembling with sheer rage. 'As I can't imagine working for you under any circumstances, I think that's superfluous information.'

'That would be a great shame. Your references impressed me with the belief that you are exactly what I'm looking for.'

'References?' Abbey questioned, her temper rising in direct proportion to his incredible cool. Last night had evidently not embarrassed him by so much as an atom, while she felt like a dupe being cruelly taunted with a massive blunder. She could not shake free of humiliating recollections of their lovemaking. She had given herself so completely: she had held nothing back and had virtually begged for his sexual possession. Those images smarted in her memory like an open wound and an unwelcome reminder of weakness and stupidity.

'I've had enquiries made and past clients speak very highly of your efficiency and devotion to detail. You have a lot of satisfied former clients out there.'

'That's good to know.' Abbey was slightly relieved by the news that he had had enquiries made, for it suggested that he was shining a professional rather than personal light onto the task of engaging her services. 'But it doesn't change my attitude. In what way did you envisage Support Systems working for you?'

'I'm planning to move my business base permanently to the UK. That is extremely confidential information, which I don't want discussed outside this room,' Nikolai spelt out, his lean, dark, devastatingly handsome face sober and serious. 'My staff are already handling the business ramifications, but I would like you to deal with the more social aspects of my move.'

'Social?' Abbey queried the term.

'As you know, my penthouse apartment here in London is convenient to this office, but if I'm to live here all the year round I will require a much larger London base, as well as a country house suitable for entertaining.'

Abbey could not believe his sheer nerve. 'You are planning to ask me to house-hunt for you?'

'A little more than that. I would prefer it if the press were kept in the dark with regard to this move for a few weeks longer.' His brilliant dark eyes gleamed in the morning sunshine filtering through the blinds. 'When the paparazzi descended on us last night and I saw the headlines this morning, it occurred to me that I could make double use of your presence in my life.' As he spoke he extended a tabloid newspaper to her.

Abbey stole a reluctant look at the headline that
screamed that the Russian billionaire had found a British
lover. She was relieved to note that a photo of them
together on the pavement outside his apartment building
the night before was so out of focus that her best friend
wouldn't have recognised her. Her name was misspelt,
her marital status incorrect and her career demoted to
the level of a clerical assistant to her brother. She cringed
at the prospect of her face and her private life being
paraded across publications that only made money from
the shock value of gossip and salacious revelations.

'Double use? I don't understand what you're sug-
gesting,' Abbey said icily, parading her lack of interest
like a banner and wishing he would take the hint.

'I want to hoodwink the press. Let them believe that
you are house-hunting because we are engaged in a
serious relationship.'

'But you don't *do* serious relationships,' Abbey
pointed out witheringly. 'When it comes to women you
have the attention span of a toddler.'

'You're not very effective in business meetings, are
you?' Nikolai breathed with sardonic bite. 'Insulting me
is scarcely good practice. Will your brother be equally
happy when he learns that you have rejected my offer?'

Abbey froze, her delicate facial bones tightening in
reaction to that blunt retaliation. She knew Drew would
be most unhappy and, bearing in mind their current financial position, she knew that he would believe he had
good cause to be angry with her.

'The press love a romance,' Nikolai pointed out.
'That would provide a useful cover story for my purchase of new homes here and conceal the fact that I'm
planning on a permanent move.'

'That's possible,' Abbey conceded curtly. 'But while I'm prepared to house-hunt for you, I'm not prepared to pretend to be flavour of the month in your bed. I would also have to tell you that I think you are the most despicable man I have ever met—'

'Do you make a habit of taking despicable men to your bed?' Nikolai quipped.

Abbey turned white as a sheet at that retaliatory crack. 'I annoyed you last night because I asked you to leave and that must have dented your macho ego. Now you want me in your pay and your power to get your own back, and the answer is no.'

'You're being very foolish. I know you can't afford to turn me down. Your family firm is dangerously overextended.'

Abbey was furious. 'That's confidential banking information. Where did you get it from?'

'My sources in financial fields are always exceptional and accurate.'

With difficulty, Abbey swallowed the ire that was threatening to choke her. She was so angry with him that containing her fury made her feel nauseous. It was impossible that she could work for him in any way, but she played for time by asking, 'What would the pretence require from me?'

'Occasional public appearances in my company, hosting a couple of parties for me, allowing me to buy you a new wardrobe and provide you with the trappings that would make the role seem more convincing.'

'As well as being at your beck and call while I look for property?'

'That, too, obviously,' Nikolai conceded.

Her violet eyes lighting up like tiny purple flames,

she viewed him in furious frustration. 'I hate you. I can't act for peanuts. I'd be a PR disaster in such a role.'

'Would you be?' Elevating an ebony brow in disagreement, Nikolai closed a hand round her narrow-boned wrist and tugged her closer to him. 'Even though you light up like a Christmas tree around me?'

'If you don't let go of me I'll thump you!' Abbey snapped at him angrily, struggling to escape his hold.

'Don't be silly,' Nikolai told her with masculine impatience.

'Get your hands off me and keep them off!' Abbey threw her free arm back to gain momentum and slapped him so hard across the cheek she was vaguely surprised that the force of it did not knock her off her feet.

Stunned, Nikolai blinked beneath the force of the blow. Across the room, Sveta stood frozen in the doorway by the little tableau before her arrested gaze. 'Nikolai?' she questioned in visible disbelief.

'*Nichivo*, never mind,' he told his assistant in Russian and dismissed her with a jerk of his arrogant dark head.

'Or do I call her back in and tell her to phone the police?' Nikolai murmured soft and low, when Sveta had departed, to Abbey, who was staring with fixed guilt and shame at the spot where his bronzed skin was reddening over his cheekbone.

'The police?' Abbey exclaimed aghast.

'You did just assault me,' Nikolai murmured silkily. 'It's been a long time since anyone struck me. My half-brothers used to beat me up all the time when I was small and these days I would prefer to fight to the death before I would allow anyone to strike me without punishment.'

'I apologise…I was completely out of order,' Abbey muttered unevenly, in a panic at the reference to the police and the risk of an assault charge, since she knew he would be quite within his rights.

Nikolai lowered his handsome dark head. 'You can kiss me better and agree to work for me. Isn't that the wiser solution?'

Abbey could not comprehend the madness that seemed to have infiltrated her brain or her life. In the past twenty-four hours she had acted like a stranger to herself and the sheer violence of her reactions was starting to scare her. Like a robot she did as she was told, pressing her peach-tinted lips delicately to the spot she had bruised while she thought about the brothers who had beaten him when he was a helpless child and found that, inexplicably, even while she hated him, her heart could ache for him as well. The musky, familiar tang of his skin flared her nostrils and she had to plant her palms against his chest to prevent herself from overbalancing.

Nikolai settled lean brown hands down on her slim taut shoulders and set her back safely from him. 'You will take the job,' he intoned, dark-as-midnight eyes telegraphing hard resolve and authority. 'And I promise you that I will give you no cause to regret the deal.'

'You don't understand how I feel,' Abbey declared fiercely.

Nikolai recognised that he had underestimated the extent of her hostility. If he wanted to see her again he had few options, because she would never willingly agree to spend time with him again. Her stubborn pride and idealistic principles exasperated him and yet he knew he could not imagine her without them.

'Naturally not. I'm not as emotional as you are,' Nikolai responded, fascinated by the fluctuating feelings that shimmered across her highly expressive face as fast as clouds in a stormy sky.

That he had recognised the depth of emotion that currently controlled her unnerved Abbey. The heights and depths of feeling attacking her usual equilibrium and swinging her first one way and then to the opposite extreme were unfamiliar to her and horribly unwelcome. She collided with smouldering dark golden eyes and her tummy flipped, her heartbeat accelerating. That fast she wanted him with a ferocious longing that she had not known it possible for her to feel. The atmosphere crackled. Her entire skin surface prickled, her nipples tightening into straining prominence, liquid heat flowering between her slender thighs. Evidently her body could not be indifferent to him: he brought out the secret slut inside her, she thought painfully.

'My aides will discuss the contract with you,' Nikolai delivered.

'With clauses regarding wardrobe and hostess duties?' Abbey queried very drily.

'No. That angle is between us alone.'

Frustration filled her. 'I'm sure a dozen women would fight for the chance to fulfil that kind of role for you. Why force it on me?' Abbey demanded.

'You have something extra, which will make you much more convincing,' Nikolai spelt out, ushering her into the room next door to where Sveta, Olya and Darya were waiting and leaving them to it.

An angry flush on her cheeks, Abbey sank down at the table next to his aides. Something extra? Extreme susceptibility to his attractiveness? In the negotiations that followed, however, she was very much at an advantage, for, while Nikolai's right-hand women might be very tough cookies, Abbey was the only one of them aware that he was not prepared to hire some other concierge firm to do his bidding. He would only settle for her and essentially that meant she could dictate her terms. And dictate them she did, refusing to give an inch in the bargaining that followed. Nikolai would be demanding and would expect instant attention, and she had no intention of allowing Support Systems to lose out; while she was devoting her time to Nikolai, she would not be in a position to take on any other clients.

Furthermore, Abbey was determined to ensure that any agreement that ensued was a businesslike one. Lifting her chin, she gathered her courage and declared, 'I want there to be a clause guaranteeing that I will not be subjected to sexual harassment during the course of the contract.'

Sveta looked even more shocked than she had been when she saw her slap Nikolai. 'I'm not sure I understand, Mrs Carmichael.'

'Nikolai will,' Abbey forecast. 'Any sexual harassment will count as breach of contract and will release me from my contractual duties.'

Sveta left the room, presumably to consult Nikolai on this unexpected demand. Abbey sat with hot cheeks beneath the combined stares of Olya and Darya, both of whom appeared affronted by her speech.

The strong lines of his lean dark face accentuated by eyes bright with satirical amusement, Nikolai appeared in the doorway. 'Let's talk, Abbey.'

Abbey rose from her chair and walked back into his office.

'I underestimated you,' Nikolai confessed with an honesty she found shockingly appealing.

'I won't work for you without that clause,' Abbey told him defensively. 'There have to be boundaries. I don't get involved with my clients.'

'But a certain amount of intimacy will be required to mislead the press,' Nikolai argued.

'I won't object to you putting an arm round me in public if it's strictly necessary, or even taking a casual kiss,' Abbey specified between clenched teeth of reluctance.

'I don't want to *take* anything from you, I want you to *give*.' Nikolai focused shimmering eyes on her, his frustration patent.

'I won't give anything more than I've just offered. Please understand and accept that what happened last night will never happen between us again,' Abbey told him tightly.

'You can't legislate against my natural male attraction to you,' he breathed in a raw undertone.

'Do you expect your female employees to tolerate sexual harassment?'

'Of course not, but you're not being fair. You were *not* an unwilling partner last night,' he reminded her starkly.

Her violet eyes dropped from his in shamed acknowledgement of that obvious truth.

'I still want you, *lubimaya*.'

'But if you also want me to agree to work for you you have to agree not to touch me again,' Abbey insisted tautly.

'Will verbal approaches still be allowed?' Nikolai asked silkily. 'Do you think you could withstand the temptation of a verbal approach?'

Abbey registered what she had unwittingly revealed: her fear that she might lack the strength of mind to reject him if he touched her again. 'Yes,' she countered doggedly.

'Then you may have your petty little clause,' Nikolai

breathed with derision. 'May it keep you warm and happy in your cold bed at night.'

Abbey lost colour but stood her ground. A few minutes later, she was back with his aides and being assured that the contract would be ready for her signature within twenty-four hours. She wondered if it was her imagination that she was now being treated with a marked note of respect.

When Sveta offered her coffee, Abbey decided to make use of the expertise available to her round the table and unfurled her notebook. 'Perhaps you could tell me what Nikolai likes in terms of housing.'

The requirements came thick and fast from all three women. Indeed the enthusiasm with which they discussed Nikolai's likes and dislikes was very revealing of their attachment to him and their admiration. 'Nikolai likes large rooms. He gets claustrophobic in small spaces,' Olya confided.

'There has to be a helipad and easy access to London. Nikolai prefers to fly himself and he enjoys the nightlife in the city,' Sveta added.

'What does he like about the countryside?' Abbey prompted.

Blank expressions met the enquiry. Apparently Nikolai had yet to demonstrate a single preference for rural pastimes—he didn't hunt, shoot or fish, nor did he cherish an interest in architecture. Darya, however, gave her useful information about his St Petersburg base. Leaving the Arlov building, Abbey embarked on a tour of the most upmarket estate agencies, gained information on several city properties and promise of further details that would be sent to her and began planning an appropriate presentation. Her mobile phone buzzed and she answered it.

It was Nikolai. 'Where are you?' he asked. 'My driver was waiting to take you wherever you wanted to go.'

'That won't be necessary—'

'Allow me to decide what is necessary.'

Abbey grimaced. 'I think I'll find it very difficult to allow you to decide anything that concerns me.'

'Where are you?'

Grudgingly she told him and he urged her to wait to be picked up.

'I'm taking you to a film premiere the day after tomorrow,' Nikolai continued. 'Sveta will be in touch with regard to your acquisition of a new wardrobe commensurate with the position you're taking on.'

'You should just get married,' Abbey informed him tartly. 'What you need is a wife, not me play-acting as a hostess in some outfit you've had to pay for.'

'I'm not the marrying kind.' His reply was icy.

A few minutes later, a limo pulled up beside her, the driver jumping out to open the passenger door to her. Abbey felt like a rubber ball being steamrollered flat by an immovable weight. She was also certain that, just like a rubber ball, she would not be able to tolerate being flattened for long. Caroline had invited her over for tea and, since it had been a couple of weeks since she had visited her brother's home, she went straight there.

Caroline's nanny opened the front door. Abbey sent an uneasy glance back at the limo, since the chauffeur had insisted that he would wait for her. Her nephew and niece, Benjamin and Alice, greeted her cheerfully and burbled on about their day at school. Abbey hugged the children and found her sister-in-law in the kitchen engaged in putting together a meal. 'You have to tell all,'

Caroline said the instant Abbey walked through the door into the cosy cluttered room.

And, to her surprise, Abbey found herself doing exactly that, although she still kept Nikolai's use of his charitable donation to put pressure on her a secret. Caroline stopped chopping vegetables for the casserole, her warm brown eyes wide and concerned. 'You slept with him?'

Abbey nodded wretchedly.

Visibly striving to conceal how surprised she was by that confession, Caroline said, 'Well, I think it's marvellous that you've finally met someone who really attracts you.'

'Even if he's a womanising billionaire?'

'The guy couldn't take his eyes off you at the fashion show. It was like he had a homing device planted on you. He's keen,' the small blond woman pronounced cheerfully. 'And why not? You're beautiful and very intelligent. Drew tells me Nikolai was on the phone first thing this morning to make an appointment to see you, so how did that work out?'

Abbey told her almost the whole story.

'I still say he's keen,' Caroline persisted. 'You've backed him into a corner. He has no other way of seeing you.'

Abbey dropped her head, her violet eyes betraying how unimpressed she was by that opinion. *Keen* was not a word she would have used to describe Nikolai Arlov. Sex was the lowest common denominator between a man and a woman and, in her estimation, the source of her appeal to Nikolai was purely sexual. He was also a male hell-bent on getting his own way, no matter what the cost or the damage.

'And there's an even brighter side to this,' her sister-

in-law continued chirpily. 'When word gets round that
Nikolai Arlov is using our services, it'll be amazingly
good free publicity and excellent for business. My
goodness—' Caroline broke off suddenly, frowning as
she looked out through the window at the limousine she
had finally noticed parked beyond the hedge. 'Did you
arrive in that monstrous vehicle out there?'

Abbey nodded uncomfortably, restrained from sharing the full content of her meeting with Nikolai by the
confidentiality he had demanded. 'Nikolai insisted I use
it while I'm working for him.'

Caroline looked amused. 'How to travel in style,'
she teased. 'You're going up in the world.'

But Abbey felt the exact opposite. Nikolai was inter-
fering with her life and she didn't care how good he
might be for business at that moment; she could only
fiercely resent his meddling. 'How are you and Drew
doing?' she prompted.

Caroline pulled a face. 'Right now, your brother seems
very worried about the business and he's still burning the
midnight oil most nights. It almost feels like he's avoid-
ing me,' she confided heavily. 'He's just not himself,
Abbey, and I don't know what's going on with him.'

Resolving to take a closer look at the accounts as
soon as she got the opportunity, Abbey went home.
Only after agreeing a pickup time with her for the following morning was the driver prepared to leave. She
found she couldn't sleep that night: Nikolai's derisive
wish that she be warm and happy in her cold bed
haunted her like a mocking laugh. She remembered the
feel of his hard muscled physique against hers and the
incredible excitement. She tossed and turned, flipping
over the pillow to find a cooler place for her hot face

to rest. Her body tingled as though she were on fire and she was so tense that when her mobile phone beeped in receipt of a text message she jumped as if thunder had rolled through the room. Worried that it might be something urgent because it was after midnight, she scrambled up with a groan and went to check her phone.

'Invite me over. I can't sleep,' Nikolai had texted her.

Rage ripped through her like a cleansing flame. She wanted to reply with something scornful, but she did not want him to know that she was lying awake as well. So she got back into bed without replying, the race of her heartbeat and the sensual tingling now banished by shame and the conviction that such responses were a shocking sign of her weak lack of self-control. As she lay dreaming up scornful replies that she might have made, she finally fell uneasily asleep.

At eight the next morning, Caroline phoned Abbey in a state and told her that Drew hadn't come home the night before and wasn't answering his mobile phone. The two women discussed whether or not it was too soon to inform the police, but before they could make a decision on that Drew finally called Caroline on her mobile and the emergency was over.

'I had a few drinks too many and slept on the sofa in my office,' her brother confided, when Abbey arrived at Support Systems later that morning. 'Caroline had no need to make such a fuss! She contacted practically everyone we know to ask if they'd seen me—'

'Your wife was worried sick about you. You should have phoned. Is that what you do when you go out these evenings—go out drinking alone?'

An angry flush on his thin face, Drew gave her a

resentful look. 'No, as it happens. I have a group of friends I usually hang out with. Mind your own business, Abbey!'

Sveta phoned and told Abbey she had an appointment at a fashion salon just before lunch. A copy of her contract had been couriered over to the legal firm Support Systems used. Abbey went through it with their solicitor and signed it. She made use of what was left of the morning to check out the properties in the City of London. Uncovering various drawbacks, she removed some of them from the list, revised her short presentation and received new information from two agents.

Sveta greeted her when she emerged from the limousine to keep their appointment and escorted her into the exclusive salon where her measurements were taken and an array of fantastic clothes was paraded by models for her benefit. Garments for every possible occasion were selected by the stylist present, who promised to locate the right accessories to go with the outfits and urged Abbey to make a personal choice from the gorgeous collection of silk, tulle and lace underwear that was laid out for her examination. In all, the acquisition of a new wardrobe entailed a display of jaw-dropping extravagance that shook Abbey to her conservative core.

'Does Nikolai often make over-the-top gestures like this?' she asked Sveta.

'Nikolai is one of a kind,' Sveta responded with diplomacy. 'I have never met his equal.'

Nikolai phoned Abbey and said he would pick her up at her apartment in an hour. 'I have a property presentation to give you,' Abbey protested.

'I'll look at it in the limo,' he promised.

'But where are we going?'

'A jeweller's. I want you to wear diamonds at the premiere tomorrow night.'

Colour in her cheeks, violet eyes bright and her red-gold hair tied back at her nape with a green ribbon, she got into his limousine clutching her laptop PC. His dark eyes brilliant, Nikolai took in her brown trouser suit and green and white polka-dotted shirt with a frown. 'You didn't dress up,' he noted.

'I'm still in work mode. Time enough to get dressed up tomorrow,' Abbey fielded, intimidated by his aura of unbridled energy and his immediate criticism. It was no consolation that he looked amazingly elegant and sexy in his tailored charcoal-grey business suit and blue silk tie. Her breath caught in her throat, her pulses starting to pound.

'You must be the only woman I've ever met who wouldn't dress up to try on diamonds.'

Abbey banged her laptop down on the space on the leather seat between them. 'Look, do you want me to go and get changed?' she asked in exasperation.

'No, you'll do.'

'You got the wrong idea about me when you saw me in that fashion show. I'm an ordinary working woman. I don't fuss about my appearance and change my clothes several times a day. I haven't got the time or the interest—I'll never be the kind of decorative woman you're used to being around,' Abbey warned him impatiently.

'But you're so beautiful that you will still outshine every woman around you,' Nikolai murmured with an amount of conviction that astonished her. 'Show me the properties you've selected.'

Abbey opened the laptop. It was soon obvious that he wasn't impressed or interested in any of the properties and her professional pride took a battering as a result. She decided to consult Sveta again.

'These properties lack the wow factor that you have in spades.' Nikolai delivered that judgement while studying her with smouldering eyes that sent a veil of pink travelling up over her cheeks.

'There will be a wow factor with the next batch,' she promised.

'It's early days,' he murmured soothingly as the limousine drew up outside an internationally renowned jeweller. 'Take your time.'

They were ushered inside and the door was locked behind them. They were the only customers in the place and champagne was served in tall fluted glasses while a display of breathtaking diamond necklaces was laid out for Nikolai's inspection. Cost never once entered the dialogue. Nikolai liked the best and only stones of the highest quality.

'Take off your jacket,' he urged her.

She removed it and undid a button on her shirt so that the neckline opened deeper to display the breathtaking sapphire-and-diamond pendant that was fastened round her neck.

'The blue complements your eyes,' Nikolai drawled softly.

Abbey stared at her reflection in the mirror arranged for her benefit. She was mesmerised by the white glittering brilliance of the diamonds against the velvet blue of the central stone. Matching earrings were brought out.

'Do you like this set?' Nikolai enquired lazily.

Abbey touched an uncertain hand to the magnificent necklace. In truth, she was so impressed that she couldn't credit that she was actually wearing such magnificent jewels. 'What woman wouldn't?' she whispered.

'You're not the average woman, *lubimaya*.' Nikolai studied the sapphire lying in the valley between her creamy freckled breasts, drawing his attention to her gloriously feminine curves. He expelled his breath in a slow measured hiss, annoyed by the sexual craving that refused to give him a moment's peace. Every time he looked at Abbey Carmichael he wanted to haul her into his arms and bury himself deep in her body. His desire was no less intense than it had been before he took her to bed and for him that was a notable first. Usually conquest and familiarity took the edge off his desire, but on this occasion it had signally failed to do so.

Abbey was relieved when the jewels were removed, packaged into cases and out of her sight. Her helpless fascination with the jewellery embarrassed and shamed her; she felt as though she had been tainted by temptation. It had never occurred to her that she might be susceptible to the corrupting power of his vast wealth, but a superficial part of her that she wasn't very proud of was already looking forward to showing off such fantastic jewels in public.

'Don't be such a puritan,' Nikolai castigated, watching her shy away from the cases. 'Don't you like beautiful things?'

Abbey couldn't help glancing at him, for she had been denying herself that pleasure since he had picked her up and the desire to wallow in visual appreciation of his stunning dark good looks and mesmeric attraction was nagging at her like a sore tooth. When he looked down at her, his black lashes rimmed his stunning eyes like silk fans and she couldn't dredge her attention from him. 'Of course I do.'

'By the way, don't wear your wedding ring tomorrow evening when you're out with me,' Nikolai told her flatly in an abrupt change of subject as they crossed the pavement to the limousine.

'It's my business whether I wear it or not,' Abbey argued, furious at that demand, which had been delivered exactly like a non-negotiable command.

'You're single. A black jet mourning ring would be more appropriate than an item of jewellery that suggests you're still married,' Nikolai responded very drily, swinging into the passenger seat beside her.

'I'll do as I like.'

Long brown fingers curled to her chin and turned her back to look at him. 'Not around me, you won't. You will do as I ask,' Nikolai asserted soft and low, dark eyes black as ice and uniquely chilling. 'I won't accept anything less than one-hundred-per-cent commitment from you.'

Abbey was outraged, but daunted by the sombre aspect to his lean, dark, handsome face. He was fighting her every step of the way, refusing to back off politely from a topic that made other people uncomfortable. Since she had already slept with Nikolai, she reasoned unhappily, her habit of wearing her wedding ring could no longer be seen as the pledge of loyalty to Jeffrey that it had once felt like.

'I'll do what I feel like doing,' Abbey countered doggedly, tossing back her head in emphasis of her power of independent thought.

'Even if it's stupid to defy me?' Nikolai demanded in a low-timbred growl of disbelief.

'Even if it's stupid,' Abbey confirmed, refusing to surrender, even though her knees were knocking together with nervous stress.

'Just for the sheer hell of it?' Nikolai queried.

Abbey nodded vigorously, pleased that he understood. She was still struggling to dampen down her anger.

'But that's illogical,' Nikolai pointed out.

Abbey knew it was and she wasn't proud of the fact. She went home with the conviction that he was teaching her things she would sooner not have known about herself. Not only was she catching herself deliberately fighting with him for the thrill of it, but she also had to face that she was not the morally upstanding and sensible person she had always believed she was. She was no more indifferent to the appeal of wonderful diamonds than any other woman. She had also managed to make a total fool of herself over a man and the knowledge stung her painfully, even though now all her energy was aimed at ensuring that she didn't repeat her mistake.

The next morning she met with Sveta at the Arlov building and showed the Russian woman the same preview of properties she'd revealed to Nikolai. Sveta mentioned a house in central London that Nikolai had often admired and advised contacting the owner with a generous offer. Abbey was taken aback by that bold suggestion, until it occurred to her that an aggressive pursuit of a spectacular property that wasn't even on the market was probably exactly the kind of approach that Nikolai would most admire. She was beginning to learn that the phrase 'thinking out of the box' might have been coined specifically to describe the Russian billionaire's high expectations.

The owner of that particular property was a Middle Eastern banker and Abbey arranged a meeting with him.

Armed with a breathtakingly good offer which had been suggested by Sveta, Abbey went into action and won the startled owner's assurance that he would consider the proposition. She left him to keep an appointment at the beauty salon where she was getting her hair done because it was the night of the premiere.

Thirty minutes after she got home in a breathless rush, the diamonds and the blue gown were delivered by one of Nikolai's security men, who announced that he would wait and travel with her as a bodyguard. She was amused by the second offering of the blue gown: Nikolai really *did* like to get his own way. This time she put it on and donned the magnificent sapphire-and-diamond jewellery and knew she had never looked better.

At his apartment, Nikolai had received his private report on Jeffrey Carmichael and had discovered that it was very well worth the reading. The dead husband whom Abbey still idolised had had very sturdy feet of clay. He wondered when he would tell her. He marvelled that nobody else had broken the bad news before him. He attempted to envisage how she would react to what he had learned and he frowned, suddenly reluctant to take on the responsibility. The truth would hurt. Did he really want to be the guy who inflicted that hurt and destroyed her romantic illusions?

He was stunned by his own indecision, for she had made her late husband his rival and in any kind of competition Nikolai's usual goal was winning whatever the cost. To be made uneasy by doubts was out of character for him. Nikolai wondered what the matter with him was. He had never been the sensitive type of male. Fate had handed him an advantage and naturally he would make the best possible use of it.

CHAPTER SIX

THE cameras went wild when Abbey climbed out of the car and rested her hand on Nikolai's arm. For an instant she froze, almost blinded by the flashes and startled by the questions flying at her from all directions.

While Nikolai's PR consultant discreetly ensured that everyone knew exactly who Abbey was, he escorted her up the red carpet into the cinema. He was proud to be with her. He thought she looked extraordinarily like a queen in the peacock-blue dress with the sapphire-and-diamond necklace and earrings flashing against the rippling mane of red-gold tresses spilling across her pale shoulders. But the very first thing he had noticed when he picked her up was that she had removed her wedding ring from her finger.

Abbey found that she was grateful for the arm that Nikolai kept at her back and the ease with which he chatted to the milling crowd of celebrities in the foyer. His assurance increased hers and, although she was madly conscious of being the centre of much curious attention and her jewellery was very much admired, she was soon laughing and smiling by his side. The film was the sort that she never went to see: a horror movie that had her sitting taut on the edge of her seat. To her embarrassment she let out a stifled shriek of fright at one point and Nikolai closed a supportive hand over hers. She glanced at him and caught the look of unholy amusement in his brilliant eyes as well as the charismatic smile that made her heartbeat perform a ridiculous somersault.

After the premiere they exchanged views on favourite films and enjoyed a lively discussion. 'You are a very entertaining companion,' Nikolai murmured levelly.

Abbey realised how much she had been talking and could hardly credit that she had relaxed to such an extent with him. 'I never go to see horror films.'

'But admit it—you enjoyed it,' Nikolai teased, curving her closer to his tall, powerful body.

'I suppose I did, in an odd way,' Abbey conceded and suddenly a smile curved her full pink mouth.

'When you smile like that I want to kiss you, *milaya*.'

Abbey froze, conscious of the number of eyes on them. '*Don't!*' she urged him. 'I'm not a fan of public displays of affection.'

'What do you like in a man?'

Abbey almost told him that she had never thought about that, but then Jeffrey's image came immediately to mind. 'Someone intelligent and confident—'

'Honest?'

'Of course,' she answered loftily.

'Faithful?'

Abbey raised a fine dark brow. 'Naturally. And of course he would have to love me.'

'You don't mention passion.'

'I'm sure, if all the other things were there, that would come, too,' Abbey countered in a dismissive tone.

'Speaking as an authority in that field, I would have to say that passion is not that easily found, *milaya*. But no relationship could be considered complete without it.'

Hot colour warming her cheeks, Abbey refused to look at him as he helped her back into the limousine, cameras flashing all around them. For that brief instant before he joined her, she felt curiously bereft. Away from his powerful presence and the aura of his high-voltage energy, everything felt flat and empty, an acknowledgement that disturbed her. She reminded herself that she could not afford to forget that she was engaging in a high-profile pretence for which he was paying Support Systems a very handsome price.

'You inspire me with immense passion,' Nikolai intoned in a roughened undertone, smouldering dark eyes as hot on her face as flames.

'It's not enough,' she told him flatly, keen to head him off before he said anything more on that controversial issue.

Nikolai bent his handsome dark head, his breath warm and moist against her temples, and she trembled. The very scent of his skin was dangerously familiar and in the space of a moment her mind was taken over by treacherous images of Nikolai in bed with her. Over her, *in* her. And, *whoosh*, all the passion she would have denied, given half a chance, roared up inside her in an uncontrollable burst of anticipation and craving. Her fingers delved into his thick black hair and she dragged his mouth down to hers because she couldn't wait one second longer to make that connection. And the instant of impact did not disappoint: the ravishing plunder of his tongue was what she wanted and needed, only it was not enough to satisfy her. The fiery urgency already pulsing through her quivering body shocked her and made her pull back from him.

'No, I'm sorry,' she breathed in an awkward rush. 'I don't want this with you—'

Lean bronzed features clenched taut, Nikolai stared down at her, his stunning eyes bright with the passion she denied. 'Yes, you *do*. Stop lying to yourself and to me.'

Abbey tilted her chin, violet eyes cool as ice water, her pride fired up in self-defence. 'I'm not lying. But I once had something a lot more worthwhile—'

'*Did* you?' Nikolai was looking at her with raw intensity and gooseflesh prickled at the nape of her neck, for there was something strangely chilling about both his look and his tone. 'Are you referring to your marriage?'

Her slender fingers coiled into angry fists, for she did not like his tone of derision. 'Don't try to make me ashamed that I still value what I had and lost!' she countered.

His hard-boned profile might have been carved from stone. He could not believe that once again she was making a comparison between him and her worthless, lying husband! It was a colossal insult and wholly eloquent of her closed state of mind. The day her husband died Abbey Carmichael had suspended all critical judgement. Surely it would be a good deed to help her to move on from the past by giving her access to the truth?

'Perhaps you didn't lose a fairy tale,' Nikolai remarked.

'And what's that supposed to mean?' Abbey hissed back at him.

'That we'll finish this discussion at my apartment.'

'I would like to know now what you are implying.'

'I think you have a very good idea, but I'll give you the proof of my words once we get there. I don't play mind games, *lubimaya*.'

Her smooth brow had furrowed. 'The…*proof*?'

In the private lift on the way up to his penthouse, he said, 'I had your late husband investigated by a private detective agency.'

Unable to credit that shocking announcement, Abbey pinned wide, startled eyes to his lean, dark, devastating face. 'Why the heck would you have done that?'

'A whim? You talked so much about Jeffrey that you made me curious about him as well,' Nikolai admitted.

'I can't believe that you invaded my personal life and violated my privacy like that!' Abbey gasped in outrage. 'It was a disgusting thing to do!'

'In this case it was more illuminating.' The forceful dark gaze that met hers contained not an ounce of remorse or apology. In the opulent hall of his apartment he left her standing and strode through a doorway. She followed him at a slower pace, her mind buzzing with conjecture and uncertainty.

Nikolai withdrew the file from the safe. Had she not challenged him again he might have retained it while he considered both his timing and his options, but he felt that she had a real right and need to know what he had discovered.

'Jeffrey was a wonderful man!' Abbey told him stridently. 'I don't care what is in that file. It won't change my mind about my husband! I loved him and he loved me. Nothing can alter those facts.'

Nikolai extended the file. 'Don't be so sure.'

Abbey snatched it off him. 'I hate you—I'll never forgive you for this! Don't you have any morals?'

'More than your husband had when he picked a naïve little schoolgirl to be his bride.'

Abbey sank down in an armchair by the door and began to scan the close lines of print. There was nothing untoward or new to her in the facts of Jeffrey's childhood and education. Then a female name that Abbey recognised leapt out at her—Jane Morrell, who had read law at Oxford with Jeffrey and who had worked in the same close circle of leading barristers. According to the enquiry agent, Jeffrey and Jane had been lovers at university, something which Abbey had not known for sure but had once suspected from the tenor of the older woman's rather acidic comments at her wedding.

Jane had married a judge, given birth to a couple of children and become Lady Jane Dalkeith long before Abbey even met Jeffrey. But what appalled Abbey as she read was the bald declaration that Jeffrey had restarted his affair with Jane while he was still in his twenties and that the couple had then continued as secret lovers for almost fifteen years. She flipped the page to be greeted with the staggering statement that Jeffrey had spent the weekend before his wedding to Abbey holed up in a Paris hotel with Jane.

'This is vile stuff and nothing but filthy lies!' Abbey spat in disgust, leaping upright. 'I don't believe any of this rubbish for one moment. I have total faith in Jeffrey.'

'Their liaison was widely known among their peers,' Nikolai informed her. 'It's a shame that nobody had the decency to tell you what was going on. Silence was cruel in the circumstances, particularly after his death.'

Abbey was shaking with rage and barely able to

vocalise or think. 'How dare you hand me this filth and try to destroy Jeffrey's reputation? How low can you sink?'

'I've never sunk as low as he did with a woman. I am always honest about what I offer and I don't cheat,' Nikolai countered drily.

'I'm not staying here discussing this with you,' Abbey told him furiously, her eyes blazing above her flushed cheeks as though someone had lit a fire inside her. 'I'm going home.'

Nikolai noticed how pale she was behind the anger. She was very loyal to her husband's memory. He thought it a great shame that the man who had inspired that deep love and loyalty had been in no way her equal. He wondered how she would feel when she was finally forced to accept the truth. Concern, a most unfamiliar sensation, gripped him on her behalf.

With trembling hands, Abbey unhooked the diamond earrings and set them down on the marble hall table. She couldn't manage the clasp on the necklace and Nikolai moved forward to help her and undid the fastening for her. 'Why are you taking them off? They're yours now.'

'You must be joking. I'm not going to accept a king's ransom in diamonds from you. I'm not one of your kiss 'n' tell girls out for everything I can get. I may hate your guts at this moment but I won't take anything from you that I'm not entitled to,' Abbey declared feverishly. 'Pay your bills to Support Systems on time and you owe me nothing.'

Nikolai surveyed her with glinting appreciation and lifted the phone. 'My driver will take you home.'

Abbey got back into the limousine like a woman sleepwalking. She studied the file afresh, fear and doubt touching her in private as she had not allowed them to

PLAY THE
Lucky Key Game

and you can get

FREE BOOKS
and FREE GIFTS!

Do You Have the LUCKY KEY?

Scratch the gold areas with a coin. Then check below to see the books and gifts you can get!

YES!

I have scratched off the gold areas. Please send me the 2 FREE BOOKS and 2 FREE GIFTS, worth about $10, for which I qualify. I understand I am under no obligation to purchase any books, as explained on the back of this card.

306 HDL EVJ5

106 HDL EVNH

FIRST NAME

LAST NAME

ADDRESS

APT.#

CITY

STATE / PROV.

ZIP / POSTAL CODE

www.eHarlequin.com

2 free books plus 2 free gifts

1 free book

2 free books

Try Again!

The Harlequin Reader Service — Here's how it works:

Accepting your 2 free books and 2 free mystery gifts places you under no obligation to buy anything. You may keep the books and gifts and return the shipping statement marked "cancel". If you do not cancel, about a month later we'll send you 6 additional books and bill you just $4.05 each in the U.S. or $4.74 each in Canada. That is a savings of at least 15% off the cover price. It's quite a bargain! Shipping and handling is just 25¢ per book, along with any applicable taxes.* You may cancel at any time, but if you choose to continue, every month we'll send you 6 more books, which you may either purchase at the discount price or return to us and cancel your subscription.

*Terms and prices subject to change without notice. Sales tax applicable in N.Y. Canadian residents will be charged applicable provincial taxes and GST. Offer not valid in Quebec. All orders subject to approval. Credit or debit balances in a customer's account(s) may be offset by any other outstanding balance owed by or to the customer. Please allow 4 to 6 weeks for delivery. Offer available while quantities last.

If offer card is missing write to: The Harlequin Reader Service, 3010 Walden Ave., P.O. Box 1867, Buffalo, NY 14240-1867

BUSINESS REPLY MAIL
FIRST-CLASS MAIL   PERMIT NO. 717   BUFFALO, NY

POSTAGE WILL BE PAID BY ADDRESSEE

NO POSTAGE
NECESSARY
IF MAILED
IN THE
UNITED STATES

HARLEQUIN READER SERVICE
3010 WALDEN AVE
PO BOX 1867
BUFFALO NY 14240-9952

touch her in Nikolai's presence. In a sudden decision she dug out her mobile phone and rang Caroline.

'Can I come and see you? I know it's late and I'm sorry but I could really do with someone to talk to,' she admitted when her friend answered her call.

'What's happened?'

'I'll tell you about it when I get there.' She opened the partition to ask the driver to take her to Caroline and Drew's home instead of her own.

'I watched you arriving at the premiere on television!' Caroline gushed as Abbey entered the lounge. 'You were in the same shot as the movie star leads. You looked amazing. But what happened to the fantastic jewellery?'

'It was only on loan and I gave it back to Nikolai.' Abbey held out the file to Caroline. 'Take a look at this and tell me what you think.'

'What on earth is it?' Jeffrey's sister questioned in lively surprise, and then when she opened it and saw the first paragraph, she exclaimed shrilly, 'Oh, my goodness! Where did you get this from?'

'Nikolai.' In the silence that followed, Abbey was so tense she could hardly breathe. She had total trust in Caroline and it was inconceivable that Caroline would not have known if her older brother was having an affair for so many years, for the siblings had always been close.

'Good heavens!' The slim blond woman in the wheelchair gasped as she read. 'How could anyone give this to you?'

Abbey's throat was so tight she didn't think she could extract a voice from it. Her entire concentration was focused on her friend and she was so tense that her knotted muscles were actually hurting her. She could not credit that doubt had entered her mind so quickly and she was ashamed that she had given way to it. She was desperate for Jeffrey's sister to tell her that the claims in the file were a pack of contemptible lies.

But as Caroline looked up, her expression appalled, Abbey felt sick and her knees gave way, forcing her to drop heavily down onto the sofa behind her. 'Tell me it's not true,' she begged.

'I only wish I could,' her friend whispered with unconcealed regret.

The silence lay thick and heavy, and Abbey felt as if she had been catapulted into a living nightmare in which everything familiar became threatening, because even her best friend could no longer look her in the eye.

'Jeffrey was having an affair...for all those years? The whole time he was with me as well?' Abbey cried.

Caroline nodded confirmation, her shrinking discomfiture with the topic painfully apparent.

Abbey felt as though a car had run over her and her very bones were being smashed to pieces inside her skin. The shock of the other woman's corroborative nod and her silence tore her apart. Caroline was her best friend and Jeffrey's sister: denial of the facts was no longer possible.

'But why did he want to marry me then?' Abbey whispered shakily. 'That doesn't make sense.'

'Jane wouldn't leave her husband and the affair was ruining Jeffrey's life. Jeffrey wanted a wife and family of his own and he could see no prospect of a future with Jane.'

A shuddering breath raked through Abbey's rigid

frame; all her romantic illusions were falling apart at once. Suddenly the whole history of her love for Jeffrey was shattering before her eyes: Jane, not she, must have been the love of Jeffrey's life. 'Why didn't you tell me? Didn't I deserve a warning?'

Caroline gave her a look of anguish. 'Jeffrey swore the affair would end before he married you and that he would be faithful—'

'Their dirty weekend in Paris only a couple of days before the wedding doesn't make the end of the affair look like it would have been a very likely development,' Abbey breathed tartly. 'Obviously Jeffrey couldn't stay away from her, so I doubt if he'd have been able to give her up entirely for my benefit.'

'You loved him so much. That drew him to you—'

'No, let's be blunt about what drew Jeffrey. I was young and foolish and I didn't know his friends or colleagues, so there was no chance that I might have heard rumours about him and Jane. I didn't ask awkward questions or expect much attention so that suited him as well. Our whole relationship was a lie, a nasty, sordid fraud, and I was the victim—'

'No...Jeffrey cared about you!' her friend protested vehemently.

'I was just the means to an end. I was to be the little housewife and mother to his children while he got his excitement, his *passion* with Jane!' Abbey snapped bitterly. 'He was using me. Does my brother know as well?'

'No. Drew had no idea, but I think your father suspected something,' Caroline admitted ruefully. 'You asked me why I didn't tell you. You were crazy about my brother and he was offering you what you appeared to want. I thought you'd be good for him and give him a chance of happiness. I honestly believed that he would make you happy as well.'

'I suppose I'd never have got him any other way,' Abbey muttered heavily, thinking of the gauche teenager she had been, easily impressed and duped by a male of Jeffrey's intelligence and sophistication.

'Stay here with us tonight,' Caroline pleaded. 'You're devastated by all this. Nikolai Arlov is a total bastard for giving you this file!'

'I don't think so. Whatever Nikolai's motives, it was past time that I knew the truth and I wish you had at least had the courage to tell me after Jeffrey died.' Averting her gaze from Caroline's discomfited face, Abbey stood up. 'Thanks for the offer, but I want to go home and come to terms with this in private.'

Abbey started trembling violently when she got back into the limo. She was hanging on to her composure by a slender thread. Tears were clogging her throat. The man she had loved had not returned her love. Jeffrey had lied to her and cheated on her and had played her for a fool. Their relationship had been an unpleasant charade that a more experienced woman might have questioned. Jeffrey had had no desire to sleep with Abbey while he still had Jane in his life. She remembered the day he had touched her red hair and asked her if she had ever thought of tinting it blond. Anguish exploded inside her like a grenade going off in a confined space. Guess who had blond hair? She remembered Lady Jane on her husband's arm at Jeffrey's funeral, long golden blond hair streaming across the shoulders of her elegant black coat, her beautiful face frozen as ice.

Abbey pressed clammy hands to her quivering cheeks.

Her best friend had stood by and watched her marry a man who was besotted with another man's wife. That awareness had ensured that Abbey had felt unable to share her innermost feelings with Caroline as she once would have done. She felt utterly betrayed. The passenger door beside her opened and only then did she realise that the journey was over and she was home.

She saw her face in her hall mirror and it scared her. Tears had smeared her eye shadow and mascara and she bore a close resemblance to a corpse in the horror film she had watched earlier. Her attention fell on the photo of her and Jeffrey on that long-ago wedding day and she snatched the frame from the wall and smashed it down on the tiled hall floor. That surge of violence shocked her to the core and she was staring down in surprise at the broken glass when the doorbell sounded.

Nikolai hammered the knocker when Abbey didn't immediately answer the bell. Relief swept him when the door finally opened and she peered out.

'I was worried about you,' he confessed in a driven undertone. 'How are you?'

'How did you think I would be?' Abbey demanded, animation and energy entering her again when she saw him. He might be the author of her evening of disillusionment, but at least she didn't have to watch her words with him. 'Happy?'

Nikolai pressed the door back and strode in, his feet crunching across broken glass. Even though the photo frame was lying face down, he recognised it and felt almost jubilant at such a demonstration of disrespect. His ambivalence towards her gnawed at him. 'I didn't want to hurt you.'

'I'm not hurt,' Abbey proclaimed.

But Nikolai could see the shock still etched in her dilated pupils and rigid bone structure. 'You need a shot of vodka.'

'No. I'm fine.' A discordant laugh fell from her lips to punctuate the strained silence. 'It'll just be a long time before I play the grieving widow again!'

Nikolai reached out in a sudden movement and gathered her into his arms.

'The bastard!' she sobbed suddenly. 'I really, *really* loved him. I thought he was the most wonderful guy in the world!'

'He didn't deserve your love.'

'He didn't want or need it!' Abbey gasped in stricken disagreement. 'He didn't even really want or need me! I was just a substitute for the woman he loved and couldn't have.'

Nikolai, who avoided emotional scenes with women like the plague, could not believe that he had got himself into such a situation. But he had found it impossible to stay away from her when he was concerned about her state of mind. Once it had entered his thoughts that she might do something foolish in her distress, he had had to seek her out and he had no intention of leaving her until he was convinced that she was all right. Right now, she was very far from being all right. She was sobbing into his chest with the abandon of a distraught child, her slim body shaking and shuddering with emotion. He smoothed her tumbled curls back from her damp brow and dug out his mobile to make a call with one hand.

'What are you doing?'

'I'm taking you home with me. I'm not leaving you here alone.'

'I'm used to being alone,' Abbey argued.

'So am I. It doesn't mean we have to like it,' Nikolai quipped, hauling open the door again and guiding her out towards the lift.

'I look a total mess and I am not sleeping with you again—'

'You're so forward,' Nikolai breathed. 'At least wait until you're asked.'

She almost laughed, and then she remembered Jeffrey again and the urge evaporated, for life as she knew it was over. She no longer had the comfort and security of looking back and wrapping herself in her fond memories of Jeffrey's love. 'I was always second best to Jeffrey,' she whispered. 'According to what his sister told me, he only settled for me because Jane wouldn't leave her husband. Everything I thought I knew about him was wrong. He even invited her to our wedding with her husband. He always talked as if he was *so* moral and there he was carrying on with someone else's wife and cheating on me throughout our engagement!'

'You're as close to being someone else's wife as I've ever got,' Nikolai remarked wryly. 'Stop torturing yourself. That affair and your marriage all ended a long time ago.'

'But I *believed* that he loved me.' Until that moment, Abbey had not appreciated just how good that belief had made her feel about herself. 'That meant so much to me. I was a lanky beanpole at school—none of the boys were interested—'

'They'd be kicking themselves if they saw you now,' Nikolai told her, pressing her head into his shoulder in a protective move when he saw the paparazzi on the pavement outside, a sharp jerk of his head telling his bodyguards to be as aggressive as they liked in shielding them from the cameras.

'I bet you were one of the popular ones at school,' Abbey commented when they had got through the crush and were safe inside his limo.

Nikolai was pouring drinks from the well-stocked bar. He handed her a shot glass of perfectly chilled vodka. 'No. My father was a crooked loan shark despised by most people. My grandfather was ashamed of him and so was I,' he admitted, only to wonder why he was telling her something that until that moment he had not even admitted to himself. His little nasty weasel of a parent had been a chronic embarrassment to him while he was growing up.

Abbey knocked back the vodka and then almost choked as it burned a liquid passage of icy fire down her throat and brought tears to her eyes. 'My word!' she spluttered as he banged her between the shoulder blades so that she could breathe again.

'Full marks for not sipping, but you didn't even give me time to make a traditional toast.'

Abbey was still thinking about what he had said. 'Why were you closer to your grandfather?'

'I lived with him until he died when I was nine years old. My father wanted nothing to do with me.'

'Why?' Abbey fixed expectant eyes on his lean dark face, her curiosity raised to a height.

'He was already married with three children when he got my mother pregnant. My grandfather took me in and raised me against my father's wishes. I think my grandfather saw it as a second chance to be a father.'

'My mother died of a heart attack a day after I was born,' Abbey confided, accepting a refill and holding it high to say. 'To a new and better understanding between us! My father never warmed to me after my mother died. He hadn't the slightest interest in me or my achievements. I was surplus. My brother was important to him because he was a boy—'

'That may be why you married an older man.'

'Nothing's that simple. I fell in love with Jeffrey.'

'But now you're going to get over that,' Nikolai intoned with cool conviction.

Shivering in the cool night air, Abbey allowed Nikolai to assist her out of the limousine and wrap her in his dinner jacket. His unexpected gallantry made her smile while his protectiveness surprised and pleased her. 'Thank you.' A car screeched to a halt a few feet away, doors flying open noisily as more men with cameras leapt out. 'Why are they still following us?'

'Press hounds have an infallible nose for a drama.'

The two shots of vodka she had had in the car made Abbey feel rather dizzy in the lift. She knew she shouldn't be with Nikolai. If ever there was a case of leaping from the frying pan straight into the fire, this had to be it, she conceded ruefully. But she was amazed that he wanted to be with her when she was in such a mood and she was equally keen not to be left alone with her depressing thoughts.

'I want a tour of your apartment,' she told him, determined to concentrate on work to protect herself from temptation. She cast his jacket down on a chair. 'It'll help me in my property search on your behalf.'

'Go where you like.' Nikolai watched her thrust off her high heels in the hall and turn in a clumsy circle that almost sent her cannoning into a sculpture. 'Vodka packs quite a kick. You should have something to eat now.'

Pangs of memory were still attacking Abbey. She was recalling how Jeffrey had pushed her away and shrinking from the cruel reason why her approaches had been unwelcome. 'You know, if a man doesn't want to sleep with you, he's either gay or he's got another woman,' she announced with the air of someone who had made an amazing deduction. 'Why didn't I get suspicious?'

Nikolai groaned out loud. 'Stop thinking about Jeffrey—you're with me!'

Abbey flipped round with something less than her usual grace. 'Well, it's not a problem you have. You never stop trying to get me into bed.'

'You need food,' Nikolai told her, directing her into the superb drawing room where an impressive selection of hot and cold snacks was laid out in readiness for them. He settled a plate into her hand and told her what everything was, for all the dishes were Russian. She settled for warm blini pancakes and caviar which she was determined to taste just once in her life.

'I need another vodka,' she announced.

'Just this once my primary objective is not to get you flat on your back,' Nikolai imparted softly. 'I think you've had enough alcohol.'

Hot pink climbed her face as she collided with his stunning dark gaze. 'I never had you picked as a nice guy,' she confided, surprised by how scrupulous he was being all of a sudden.

'I'm not, but I'm the guy who gave you that file.'

She couldn't tell him she was grateful because every time she thought about what she had found out it was as if someone had slashed her with a knife and another whole slew of fond memories would be destroyed. Even worse were the vague memories of inconsistencies that now fitted her new awareness of Jeffrey as a deceiver, who had lied about loving her and hurt her self-image by making her feel insecure about her ability to attract him.

While she wandered aimlessly round the room admiring Nikolai's spectacular views over London, she saw her face in a mirror and almost died with embarrassment on the spot. How on earth had she contrived to forget her messy make-up? 'I need to clean up—I look awful!' she exclaimed.

Nikolai directed her to the cloakroom, which was roughly the size of her whole apartment and equipped to fulfil a woman's every need. She wiped her eyes clean and washed her hands free of crumbs before lingering to touch up her make-up, reasoning that feeling down didn't mean she had to give up her pride in her appearance, particularly not with a male as gorgeous as Nikolai around…

CHAPTER SEVEN

'I'M going to take a look around the apartment now,' Abbey informed Nikolai airily when she rejoined him.

'It's just a functional space, bought for a convenient location,' Nikolai said dismissively.

Abbey looked at the home office where he worked with interest, but it was the master bedroom suite that she was truly most curious about. She whooped at first glimpse of the massive bed and could not resist taking a running jump to bounce on it. His attention welded to her every move, Nikolai came to a halt just inside the door with a wry smile on his lean, bronzed face as he watched her.

Abbey looked up at the mirror on the ceiling above the bed and winced. 'Such a playboy cliché,' she scolded. 'Is that really why you worked so hard to become massively wealthy? All the beautiful women it would put within your reach?'

The faintest hint of colour scored Nikolai's stunning cheekbones as he watched her. She was a vibrant figure in the blue dress he loved, her glorious red hair rippling round her delicate face and her violet eyes shining with amusement. 'No, I wanted to be rich so that nobody could ever push me around again.'

Abbey couldn't laugh at that confession. She thought about the half-brothers who had beat him up, and flinched. By the sound of it, his childhood had been very low on love and caring. It was little wonder that he had grown into a tough and ruthless adult, who believed he had no need for ties based on the more tender emotions, and who preferred to make money his most meaningful avenue of communication.

She investigated the panel of buttons on the wall and experimented, switching on and dimming the lights, opening the curtains and lifting a massive television screen and entertainment centre into view only to drop it out of sight again. She started to giggle. 'I'm behaving like a toddler let loose on a computer keyboard, aren't I?'

Nikolai strolled across the room. Overpowered by her giggles, Abbey was in a helpless heap on his bed. 'This wasn't quite how I pictured you in here,' he acknowledged.

'You'll never give me vodka again,' Abbey forecast.

Nikolai sank down on the bed beside her. She felt his presence and rolled over onto her back to gaze up at him. 'I like looking at you,' she told him helplessly. 'But that's just sex, isn't it?'

Lean brown fingers gently smoothed the tumbled coppery curls back from her pale brow. 'I like looking at you, too...'

There was an odd, almost wistful note in his dark, deep voice that quivered down her taut spine. She stared at him and suddenly she wanted him with a hunger that clawed at her like a physical pain. 'Kiss me,' she told him. 'In Russian my answer would have to be *Nyet*.'

'*No?*' Abbey gasped, translating that negative in open astonishment. 'Because of the contract we signed?'

'Stuff the contract,' he breathed, the pad of his fore-finger tracing the tantalising pout of her full lower lip and slipping inside to probe when she opened her mouth.

In punishment for that teasing act, Abbey bit his fin-gertip and he withdrew it. 'So, stop mucking around and get on the bed,' she told him bluntly.

A reluctant smile slashed his beautiful mouth. 'When did you become so dominant?'

'I learnt it from you,' Abbey fielded, breathless beneath the hard sensual heat of his appraisal and the glow of his approval, her heart beating so fast and urgently that it felt as if it were lodged in her throat. 'It gets you what you want.'

'When you were sober, you said you didn't want this, *lubimaya*.'

The reminder was as unwelcome as the physical re-luctance she sensed in him. She craved his wide sensual mouth like a drug and he was turning her down nicely, it was true, but a rejection was still a rejection and deeply wounding in the frame of mind she was in. She twisted away and pushed her mortified face into a pillow. He had taught her to believe that he found her downright irresistible and the rebuff, for whatever reasons, hurt and reminded her of Jeffrey's lack of en-thusiasm. 'You don't want me the way you said you did,' she condemned tightly.

Nikolai swore in Russian below his breath. She was driving him insane. There she was on his bed, looking more seductive than any fantasy, and he couldn't touch her because he didn't want to be accused of having taken advantage of her in the morning. 'You know that's not true—'

'Or maybe this is a revenge kick. I rejected you, so

now you're rejecting me just when I can't cope with it!'
That final accusation emerged in a semi-wail as tears got
the better of Abbey, whose desirability factor now felt
at an all-time rock-bottom low.

'How can you not know how wrong you are?'
Nikolai flipped her slim body over as if she weighed no
more than a toy and glowered down at her, his tawny
eyes smouldering. He carried her hand to his groin to
prove his point.

Abbey blinked in surprise at that rather graphic demonstration of male interest. Her fingers lingered on the
bold outline of his erection, caressing him through the
fine wool of his trousers. *'Oh,'* she said with a wealth
of feminine meaning in her voice, satisfaction flaring
inside her as she acknowledged his impressive arousal.

'You're torturing me,' Nikolai groaned.

'I want to make love to you,' Abbey confessed,
leaning over him to undo his belt and run down his zip.
He slid off the bed and began to peel off his clothes for
her. She watched him strip, responsive heat flaring in
sensitive places as his rampantly male and athletic
physique emerged from his clothing. He was hugely
aroused and in that instant, when his eager impatience
made her feel like the most desirable woman in the
world, there was nothing she would not have done for
him. Although she was a little short on actual expertise,
her sheer enthusiasm more than made up for it. She
kissed and caressed her path across his washboard-flat
stomach. His fingers slid into her hair to hold her to him.
She loved touching him and she adored it when he
moaned and trembled beneath her enthusiastic caresses.

'Come here,' he told her urgently, finally dragging
her up to him to claim her luscious lips with a raw

driving hunger that left her dizzy. 'You're living proof that fantasies can come true, *milaya moya*.'

Still shocked by her own audacity, Abbey had little idea of what had come over her, only that for the first time in a very long time she had felt free to be herself. 'Don't tell me stuff like that if you don't mean it,' she warned him.

Nikolai wound long fingers into her tousled tresses. 'And don't you change your tune when you get out of my bed again,' he traded in steely admonition. 'No more blowing hot and cold.'

'Yes, boss.' Abbey laughed as he unzipped her dress, and then a comical expression of dismay froze her lovely face.

'*What?*' Nikolai demanded.

'I'm sleeping with a client,' she said in horror.

'You haven't yet, but I'm living in a lot of hope,' Nikolai confessed facetiously, tugging her up against him to unhook her delicate blue bra, his hands rising instantly to cup her full breasts with an earthy sound of satisfaction. He pressed his lips to the sensitive nape of her neck while his skilful fingers teased her straining pink nipples.

'I don't think you're going to be disappointed.' Her voice was all over the place because she couldn't hold it steady. She was out of breath and her heart was racing; excitement was already overwhelming Abbey. Just thinking about the pleasure about to be unleashed on her eager body sent her from cool to hotter than hot in the space of seconds.

Nikolai laid her down against the pillows like an artist arranging a tempting display. His spectacular dark golden eyes raked over her with unhidden heat and appreciation and it was balm to her squashed ego to recognise the strength of his desire.

'I'd like to keep you in bed for at least a week.'

Her body pulsed with longing at the mere mention of such an indulgence.

'So, the deal is…' Nikolai breathed huskily, kissing a haphazard path down over her quivering body and teasing at the shallow indentation of her navel. 'The deal is that before I go any further, you agree to stay here with me every night—'

'*All* week?' Abbey gasped, slender fingers smoothing his black hair in a caressing motion that came as naturally to her as if she had been doing it all her life.

'*All* week and every night for two weeks,' Nikolai emphasised with determination.

'Two weeks? And if I say no?' she enquired in a small voice.

Nikolai smoothed a carnal hand up over her slender shaking thigh to stroke his fingertip over the most sensitive spot in her entire body and provoke a startled gasp of response from her. 'Say no and you get turfed out of bed and sent home in disgrace for behaving like a one-night stand.'

An incredulous giggle at that threat was dragged from Abbey. 'You're blackmailing me with sex?'

His fingertip inscribed an erotic circle of unbearable sensation and her hips jerked and her lips parted on a pleading whimper that she couldn't hold back. 'Yes. It's a novelty to be with a woman who can't be bought with diamonds. So what's your answer?'

'Yes, it has to be yes.' If he had turfed Abbey out of bed just then she would have screamed with frustration. She couldn't resist him. His lean hands parted her thighs and he pressed his mouth to her stomach and she trembled at the touch of his lips and his tongue on her sensitised skin. She remembered her wretched sense of betrayal earlier and marvelled that she was now in Nikolai's bed and content to be there. As his exploration travelled in a much more intimate direction, shock snaked through her in a rousing wave. She protested; he ignored her. She stopped thinking, she stopped arguing, because her very senses were suddenly centred on the tender flesh at the heart of her womanhood and the exquisite torment of sensation he was using to win her acquiescence. Her excitement climbed until the first flutters of orgasm low in her stomach grew into a hurricane of meltingly sweet pleasure that whirled her up as high as the heavens and made her cry out his name.

'And now it's my turn again,' Nikolai breathed unevenly, tugging her up and rearranging her on her knees in front of him.

His hands hard on her hips, he entered her slick wet heat with irresistible force. She gasped at that bold entrance, wildly aware of his every tiny movement. He reached down to fondle her breasts and stroke the taut peaks to pouting buds of tingling responsiveness. His powerful thrusts were fiercely thrilling and she was in a state of such extreme stimulation that she was totally out of control. He drove her to another shattering climax and she collapsed down on the bed, her senses spinning from the overload of excitement and her body exhausted by the abandoned response he had extracted.

He turned her over, framed her hectically flushed face with his hands and kissed her breathless. Struggling to breathe normally again, she responded by wrapping her arms round him and hugging him tight. Emotion was surging through her in a scorching volley and she couldn't define what it was or restrain it. His passion exhilarated her to the very depths of her being, but what made her cling was the fact that in his arms she felt amazingly special and safe.

Nikolai tensed; he hadn't expected affection from her, but she was snuggling into him like an extension of his own body. In another moment he would go for a shower to cool off, but, in the meantime, he would let her hug him to her heart's content. He was quietly confident that while she was fully engaged in kissing and hugging him she wasn't thinking about Jeffrey the cheat.

Abbey was still revelling in the sensual touch and taste of Nikolai. The minute a thought about her late husband tried to intrude she shut it out. She told herself that she was moving on, *finally* moving on. She supposed embarking on an immediate affair with a notorious womaniser was a very bad move to make in the circumstances, but the damage was done, and when Nikolai looked at her or touched her free choice truly didn't seem like one of her options. Something that had nagged at her earlier returned to her mind and curiosity prompted her to try to clarify the issue.

'When you were talking about your father and grandfather you never once mentioned your mother,' Abbey remarked abruptly.

Nikolai tensed and then pulled free of her hold entirely. 'No, I didn't, did I?'

Abbey stiffened and turned to look at him. His devastatingly handsome face was set as cold as ice and she reacted angrily to the feeling that she was being snubbed. 'I gather that's a conversational no-go area as far as you're concerned. It's a bit of a joke, that, when you're fresh from paying someone to investigate and report on my late husband's every move from birth!'

'My background is not something I talk about,' Nikolai growled, tossing back the sheet he had pulled over them while they lay there.

'I didn't particularly want to talk about my late husband's undying love for another woman tonight either,' Abbey snapped back at him without hesitation, 'but nobody respected *my* privacy!'

Nikolai shot her a murderous look of censure. She had the tact of an elephant. Others respected his reserve. He wasn't accustomed to having to answer awkward questions. 'I'm going for a shower.'

'Get Sveta to draw up a list of subjects I must avoid… otherwise it's likely to be an endurance test of a fortnight!' Abbey muttered feelingly, cut off by his attitude. 'You react like offended royalty.'

Nikolai showered, angrily recalling the fact that he had planned to take her into the shower with him, but now she had spoilt the mood with her nosy questions. *Offended royalty?* His nostrils flared. He was not that spoilt or that far removed from ordinary people. How could he be when he had once known what it was to go hungry and cold? But then, how could Abbey have known what not to say when she had no idea of what his background was? His own curiosity had made him plunder her private life for answers without hesitation, he conceded grimly.

Tears flooded Abbey's eyes all too easily. She knew she was being over-sensitive, but it had been a long and emotionally exhausting day. The last thing she needed just then was the discovery that she had become intimate with a guy ready to freeze her out for the most minor infraction of his rules.

Without warning, the bathroom door shot open again to frame Nikolai's big powerful frame in the doorway. With wet black hair plastered to his well-shaped skull, he was dripping water everywhere. 'Join me in the shower and I'll tell you what you want to know, *lubimaya moya.*'

An involuntary smile drove the tension from her compressed mouth. She wondered if he thought that more sex was the answer to every problem and reckoned that he was basic enough to think that. But she was determined not to blow hot and cold, as he had put it, and, having committed herself to a course, she was not one to turn back. She got out of bed and although it was a challenge for her to walk naked across the depth of that room in front of him, she did it with her head held high.

'I love your body,' Nikolai husked in reward as he snatched her up off her feet and carried her into the shower with him.

His powerful uncompromising masculinity stirred Abbey beyond bearing. She linked her hands round his neck and stretched up and he accepted her invitation with passionate force, crushing her ripe pink mouth beneath the hungry demand of his. That fast, that easily, Nikolai lit a fire of longing inside her again. His rigid erection butted against her belly and he lifted her with easy strength, his hands cupping her hips as he held her over him. 'So much for the shower I was promised,' Abbey muttered.

'I can't stop wanting you,' Nikolai growled and something of his surprise and resentment of that apparent fact was etched in his lean hard-boned features. 'I have you once and it's not enough.'

And she wondered why she was complaining when

she liked that, when indeed she gloried in having that power over him. He was kissing her with ravenous desire when he tumbled her down on top of the towels he had thrown on the floor. But just as he established her readiness, he released her again with a groan of impatience and vaulted upright to return to the bedroom. 'I need protection…'

Even as her restive hips pressed against the hard floor below her, seeking some form of relief from the tormenting ache he had roused, she appreciated the fact that he wasn't taking any risks. When he returned to her he found the taut jut of her nipples and the slick wet heat between her thighs with his mouth and his skilful hands and reduced her to honeyed, purring compliance before sliding over her and sinking into her and introducing her to the wickedly exquisite pleasure all over again. In the aftermath of satiation, he kept her close and she shut her eyes, so tired and drained she was ready to sleep.

'I don't know who my mother is. I don't even know her name. I know nothing about her,' he admitted gruffly.

Her eyes stung with tears of emotion, her heart swelling with sympathy on his behalf and understanding of why he preferred not to discuss his background. 'That must be very tough for you,' she said in a wobbly voice.

Nikolai lifted his tousled dark head and looked down at her and saw the sheen of moisture on her cheeks. Shocked that she was distressed on his behalf, he stroked her cheekbone in a soothing gesture. 'I'm a tough guy. I'm used to it.'

'Were you an abandoned baby?'

Nikolai shook his head. 'No. My grandfather chose to take me on. He was a diplomat and he had to be inventive in how he registered my birth when he took me back into the Soviet Union. The name on my birth certificate was a fake and he told me that when I was a kid, and that he would explain everything when I was old enough to understand. Unluckily for me he died very suddenly and he took the secret to the grave with him.'

Abbey marvelled that his father had not been prepared to fill in the gaps for him and only then understood just how bleak his experience of family ties must have been as a child. 'It doesn't matter who brought you into the world—it's who you are now that's important,' she told him chirpily.

'What a great thought for the day!' Nikolai mocked, gazing down at her and noticing how translucent and pale her skin was and how shadowed her eyes were. 'You're exhausted.'

'Hmm...' Abbey mumbled and she didn't remember another thing until she woke up the next morning to the distinctive and familiar sound of her mobile phone ringing.

'Ignore it,' Nikolai urged, his arms tightening round her.

Abbey was warm and unbelievably comfortable. She wanted to snuggle, not move away, but her conscience was twanging.

'I can't ignore it. It's probably Caroline. I was upset when I left her last night.' With a rueful sigh, Abbey snaked away from Nikolai and scrambled up.

Her phone was in her clutch bag, which she had left lying on the dressing table the night before. As she had assumed, the call that she had missed had been from her sister-in-law. Calling Caroline back only took a moment. As it was still only six-thirty in the morning she was surprised that the subject was work-related. Evidently, however, Mr bin Hashim, the Middle Eastern banker who owned the house she was trying to acquire for Nikolai, had tried to contact her the night before to arrange an early meeting with her that very morning. It was imperative that she did not miss that appointment and offend the man.

'I've got an appointment and I haven't even got any clothes to wear!' Abbey exclaimed, and then stared in horror at her reflection in a wardrobe mirror for her hair was a fluffy nest of wildly messy curls.

'I'll send out for clothes for you. I want you to stay and have breakfast with me.'

'I *can't*. This is work,' she responded in a tone of urgent appeal.

'I'm holding a massive party here tomorrow night and you're going to be my hostess. Isn't that work as well?' Nikolai traded unanswerably.

'This is a very important appointment,' Abbey groaned.

Nikolai was already using the phone by the bed to rap out instructions in Russian. He held out a shapely brown hand. 'Come back to bed...'

Abbey went pink and averted her attention from him. She was as stiff as a board and walking was a challenge. 'I couldn't...er...comfortably,' she told him awkwardly.

Comprehension lit Nikolai's keen gaze as he registered that he had been too demanding. 'I'll settle for just holding you, *lubimaya*.'

'Even if I can't stay for breakfast?' Abbey was already yanking a comb with painful strokes through her hair in the bathroom.

'If you don't I'll be angry.'

Within half an hour a brand-new outfit was delivered to the bedroom and she was able to don the black trouser suit and blue silk shirt quickly. Nikolai, magnificent in a navy pinstripe business suit worn with a fashionable dark shirt and light tie, accompanied her down to the main hall. 'I'll see you at eleven in my office,' he told her drily. 'If you don't show, I'm sacking you.'

'For goodness' sake, Nikolai,' Abbey began in frustration. 'Don't be so unreasonable—'

'Polite requests are wasted on you,' Nikolai countered, dark eyes hard as granite.

His manservant was in the act of letting Sveta in through the front door. The beautiful elegant blonde strolled in with a business case and greeted them both. Abbey was hugely embarrassed to be found in Nikolai's apartment at that hour of the day, a sensation that was not dimmed by the obvious tension in the air that she could see the other woman picking up on.

'I'll see you later,' she told Nikolai in a rush, reluctant to say anything more personal with an audience present and even more reluctant to confide that when she said later, she meant *very* much later.

Sveta said something in Russian and Nikolai translated. 'The paparazzi are waiting outside in droves.'

Abbey's face turned a dulled red. The very idea of advertising the reality that she had spent the night with Nikolai for the benefit of the international press made her cringe. In his world, she thought unhappily, privacy seemed a virtual impossibility.

His security team saw her safely into the waiting car. She tortured herself with self-loathing all the way to her appointment with the banker. She was a woman who always liked to control her own destiny and she had embarked without thought on an affair with a male who was demonstrating a disturbing desire to control every hour of her day. She was furious with Nikolai on that score and had every intention of telling him so. Mr bin Hashim had decided to sell the house, which improved Abbey's mood, until she called in at Support Systems where her brother chucked a tabloid newspaper down on her desk and demanded to know what was going on.

Abbey compressed her mouth when she saw the photo of herself with Nikolai, the distress on her face obvious. It had been taken outside her apartment building the night before. 'It wasn't Nikolai who upset me—'

'I'm aware that Jeffrey's been exposed as a love rat—yes, Caro finally spilled the beans last night. But aren't you asking for trouble getting mixed up with Nikolai Arlov on the rebound?'

'I thought you were delighted and convinced that he'd be good for business.'

'I don't want to see you getting hurt again.'

On the rebound, Abbey repeated inwardly as she left the office to meet with Nikolai. Even though it was six years since Jeffrey's demise, she supposed that phrase most accurately described what was happening to her. Knocked off balance and hurt and humiliated by the unlovely truth about Jeffrey, she had gone overboard when Nikolai had made her the target of his attentions.

On the balance side, however, she was quick to console herself with the reflection that she had no naïve expectations of Nikolai Arlov. She did not have any kind of a future with him. She was well aware that Nikolai was only interested in a short-term affair and then in all likelihood she would be history by the end of the month. It was surely no coincidence that he had specified she spend two weeks of nights with him? Was that as long as he imagined his interest would last? She had grown up a lot since Jeffrey, she told herself bracingly. There was no way that she was about to fall madly in love with Nikolai!

CHAPTER EIGHT

ABBEY was ushered into Nikolai's presence the very moment she arrived on the top floor of the Arlov Industries building. It was fifteen minutes past eleven o'clock.

'You're late,' Nikolai breathed with sardonic bite.

'I'm here. Don't be petty,' Abbey told him, lifting her chin in a direct challenge. 'And I think you'll be pleased that I kept that other pressing appointment this morning. It was for your benefit.'

Nikolai watched in silence as she brought up pictures of the property on her laptop. His ebony brows pleated in immediate recognition. 'How did you find out?'

'That you admired the house? All thanks go to Sveta. She told me about it, suggested a price and discussed tactics. She was very helpful,' Abbey told him frankly.

Nikolai was hugely impressed by her honesty and her attitude. She knew how to network and she was willing to share the praise and rewards of a successful outcome.

'If you want the house, it's yours,' Abbey imparted. 'You have an invitation to view it this afternoon if you like.'

'Yes, I will, but I already know I want the house. I attended a party there once. It was held by the previous owner after he had carried out extensive renovations.'

Abbey ran through the house's many attributes from the number of bedrooms to the massive garaging space and the basement swimming pool.

'You've done spectacularly well,' Nikolai delivered, closing his hands over Abbey's and drawing her to him for emphasis. 'I'm very pleased.'

Abbey connected with his gorgeous dark eyes and her tummy somersaulted as if she were on a big dipper ride. Breathing normally was suddenly a challenge. His high voltage sexuality engulfed her like a dangerous force field and memories assailed her. Only hours had passed since she had shared intimacies with Nikolai that she had never dreamt she would share with any man. Soft colour warmed her cheeks and heat curled low in her pelvis, making her legs tremble.

'You want me, *lubimaya*,' Nikolai pronounced with satisfaction.

Glancing away, Abbey took a measured step back from him. 'Let's keep that aspect of our relationship out of the office,' she urged tautly. 'It makes me feel uncomfortable.'

Nikolai frowned. 'I don't like rules and restrictions.'

Abbey forced a smile. 'But there's a right way and a wrong way of doing everything and I like to be sensible.'

'Passion should be cherished,' Nikolai countered.

'In private. It's too public here,' she argued daringly. 'Tell me about tomorrow night's party.'

'Sveta did a breakdown of the guest list.' Nikolai handed her a small file. 'I think she's made some appointments for you as well.'

As Nikolai employed the phone Abbey was ready to gnash her teeth in frustration. Meeting Nikolai's demands really was turning into a round-the-clock occupation. The useful information on various important business guests was paired with a list of beauty appointments that threatened to take up a good part of the following day.

Abbey slapped the sheet down on Nikolai's desk. 'I can't keep up with this and you and work as well. There aren't enough hours in the day! You are a very unreasonable man. I'm not a trophy girlfriend! And I flatly refuse to be made to feel like a kept woman. I've got better things to do with my time than spend the day being groomed like a pet poodle before I can be seen out with you in public!'

'Exactly what are you so angry about?'

Purple eyes luminous with furious frustration, Abbey spread both arms in a helplessly expansive gesture. 'You're taking over my whole life!'

'Am I? You left my bed at six-thirty this morning and didn't even stay to breakfast,' Nikolai reminded her.

'And you're still furious about that even though I was meeting with the owner of the house you want to buy?' Abbey demanded hotly. 'Does that strike you as reasonable behaviour?'

Nikolai grasped one of her slender hands in a firm hold and used his strength to inexorably pull her closer. 'I want you with me, *milaya moya*. What's wrong with that?'

The deep, dark note in his accented drawl thrummed down her sensitive spine like a sensual wake-up call. Ensnared by the brilliance of his dark, deep-set gaze, she snatched in a quivering breath. 'Nothing, but—'

'And the beauty appointments and the clothes? I don't want you to be made to feel inadequate beside my well-groomed guests. To date, you haven't even been at home long enough to have your new wardrobe delivered,' Nikolai reminded her. 'You demand too much of yourself. Give your keys to Sveta and she'll organise delivery for you.'

Abbey felt uneasily as though the ground beneath her once sensible feet were being sliced away, leaving her teetering on the edge of an abyss. He wasn't letting her reinforce her independence. Nor was he giving her space to withdraw. His thumbs were massaging the delicate skin of her inner wrists and her senses were singing. Her body was awakening to his proximity with a shameless range of physical responses that shook her. Her mouth was dry, her heartbeat accelerating at a crazy rate of knots. Her brain was urging her to step away from him as she had earlier, but less scrupulous responses were stronger. She felt as mesmerised as a rabbit caught in car headlights. She braced a hand against the rock-hard wall of his chest and leant in closer.

The evocative aroma of his skin hit her like a shot of adrenaline and made hunger skyrocket inside her. The strength of her desire to get closer, to feel his beautiful mouth take hers again, to feel the weight of him over her, shocked her rigid.

Nikolai surveyed her dazed face with cool satisfaction. He wondered why it was that when other women looked at him like that he wanted to ditch them, but when Abbey stood there fighting not to look at him like that he simply wanted to smash her self-control and encourage her to cling. 'Stop fighting this,' he urged.

'I have to.' The strength of her own physical response to him, allied to the see-sawing state of her emotions, scared Abbey. 'I must have my own life, my own space—'

Long fingers delved into her hair to tip up her face and her breath tripped up in her throat, anticipation leaping through her in a wild surge. He covered her mouth, his tongue darting deep into the moist interior beyond, and she shuddered violently, a stifled whimper wrenched from her struggling lungs. 'No, not here,' she protested.

Nikolai lifted his arrogant dark head. He ached for her. He couldn't keep his hands off her or his thoughts on business. Tawny eyes smouldering he hauled her up into his arms and strode to the chair behind his desk, sinking down with her on his lap.

'Nikolai…' Abbey argued in a ragged plea.

Shimmering eyes hotly intent on her, he laid his fingertips against her reddened lips to silence her. 'I am not made of stone…'

Fiercely aware of his arousal, Abbey was engulfed by the demanding heat of his mouth in a kiss that fired her every skin cell with awareness. Her fingers smoothed the roughened skin of his jaw line where stubble was beginning to mar the close shave he had had earlier that day. The familiar scent and the sensual feel of him sent her pulses racing. As he unbuttoned her shirt she was remembering the night that had passed. He had woken her up a couple of times, his desire for her flatteringly intense and his sexual expertise compelling. Then, as now, his sheer passion and unbridled masculinity exhilarated her.

Nikolai bent her back over his arm to plunge his mouth down on the pouting pink nipple he had uncovered for his pleasure. Abbey looked down at the ripe curves of her bare flesh and shame overwhelmed her. She flung herself off his lap and began to right her clothing in a series of jerky desperate movements. '*Not during working hours!*' she breathed shakily.

'Where's your sense of adventure?' Nikolai growled,

furious with her for once again limiting his pleasure in her as a lover. 'What does it take to make you break the rules?'

Love and commitment, she might have told him, for only then would she have had the trust and confidence to respond to him regardless of boundaries. But Abbey knew that neither love nor commitment was on offer, which severely limited any desire on her part to break rules. 'I have to get back to the office—'

'You could join me for lunch and we could go on from there to the house viewing,' Nikolai breathed curtly, already foreseeing a negative answer in the tense down curving of her generous mouth.

Abbey was convinced that lunch would end up being a polite blanket term for a bout of sex somewhere and she cringed for herself when she felt a pulse of wickedly responsive heat throb in her pelvis. 'You want me to view the house with you?'

Nikolai dealt her a sardonic appraisal. 'Of course.'

'Give me a time and we'll meet there.'

Nikolai was like a brooding thundercloud when Abbey departed after a brief chat with Sveta. Abbey was uneasily conscious that she had dissatisfied and disappointed Sveta's employer in every possible way. Her insistence on striving to be professional during the hours of daylight pleased her Russian lover as much as a slap in the face. She was beginning to get the message about what he wanted from her. He didn't handle rejection well. He expected to come first in her life in every way and in every situation. Argument, disagreement, working ethics that interfered with his sex life and independence were all very unpopular responses.

On the way back to the office, Abbey received an urgent call from her PA about a man waiting to see her, who insisted that it was important that he speak to her rather than to her brother. New clients did occasionally arrive at Support Systems with very set ideas and required tactful handling. With a sigh, Abbey picked up her messages from her PA's desk and invited the smartly dressed older man in reception to come into her office.

'I'm Abbey Carmichael, Mr...Bailey. Is that correct?' Abbey prompted as the man took a seat.

'Yes. Don Bailey. I won't keep you long, Mrs Carmichael. I don't know how much you know about your brother's debts, but I'm afraid the operation that I represent is not prepared to wait indefinitely for settlement.'

Abbey's face had tightened with surprise and uncertainty. 'Debts? My brother's debts?' she queried in astonishment. 'Apart from the obvious fact that I'm not at liberty to discuss anything pertaining to my brother, I can't understand why you've asked to see me.'

'Your brother's mucking us about and we want our money, Mrs Carmichael. It's a big chunk—over one hundred and twenty thousand pounds at the most recent count.'

Abbey had to lean back against her desk to stay upright on legs that suddenly felt hollow and weak. She could barely believe what she was hearing. 'One hundred and twenty thousand pounds?' Feeling out of her depth, she reached for the phone. 'Look, I'll call my brother in and you can talk to him—'

In a sudden unexpected move, Don Bailey closed his hand over hers to prevent her from making the call. 'No, that's not a good idea, Mrs Carmichael. Drew will be annoyed I've come here to see you, but we've been exceptionally patient with him. Unfortunately we can't continue to be so understanding and matters are likely to take an unpleasant turn if the cash isn't forthcoming very soon.'

Abbey snatched her hand from beneath his repulsive clasp and backed away, her skin clammy with fright and nervous tension. 'Was that a threat, Mr Bailey?'

'It's whatever you choose to make of it,' he replied with a menacing lack of concern on that score. 'Drew's a gambler and, like many another, while he's happy enough to win, he's in no hurry to pay his dues when he loses. But make no mistake, your brother does have to pay his debts and in full.'

Abbey swallowed the lump of extreme anxiety in her throat. Had Drew been gambling? All those nights he had come home late? Was this why he was so stressed out and short-tempered? Was it possible her brother could owe such a huge sum of money? And if he did, what were they going to do about it?

'Now, I had a choice today about whether I should come and see you or go to see Drew's wife.'

Abbey felt ill at the thought of this horrible man tackling her friend, Caroline. 'No, you did the right thing asking for me.'

'I thought so, too. You are a partner in this business as well and, if you don't mind me mentioning it...' Don Bailey gave Abbey a meaningful look '...according to the newspapers, you are also very friendly with a Russian billionaire who could easily settle all your brother's problems for him.'

Abbey could not conceal her distaste at that suggestive sally. 'Let's leave that friendship out of this!'

'Whatever you say. After all, we only want what's owing to us and we don't care who pays it or how. But the debt *must* be settled and very soon before we lose our patience,' the older man completed with an ominous look. 'Is that understood, Mrs Carmichael?'

Abbey was pale and she felt queasy. 'Yes.'

From a rear window she watched Don Bailey climb into the Mercedes parked in the staff car park. There were a couple of other men waiting in the vehicle and although at that distance it was hard to be certain, she suspected they were the same grim-looking men whom she had seen before and whom Drew had pretended were potential customers. Abbey spared the group one last troubled glance before going straight into Drew's office and telling him about the visit. As Don Bailey had forecast, her brother was furious.

'Look, it doesn't matter that he talked to me. All I want to know is—is it true? And do you owe that ghastly man one hundred and twenty thousand pounds?'

His angry flush receding to leave a greyish pallor, her brother settled down heavily behind his desk again. 'Yes…yes, it's true.'

Abbey was appalled by the story Drew went on to tell her. He had first gone to the casino where Don Bailey worked as what her brother termed a 'heavy' to play the tables with a friend. Winning money at that first visit, he had soon returned and had quickly found it impossible to stay away.

'You might as well know the worst. I've drawn thousands and thousands of pounds from the business to finance my gambling habit and lost every penny of it. I've mortgaged my family's home for every penny I could get and lost that as well. Ever since last winter I've been trying to pay off massive losses. But I haven't once played since then,' Drew declared. 'I'm a compulsive gambler and now I attend Gamblers Anonymous meetings every week to help me stay in control of my addiction. Unfortunately I wised up and joined too late to stop myself from dragging us all down into financial ruin.'

Abbey was devastated to learn that her big brother, whom she trusted and loved, had stolen from both her and his family by secretly bleeding vast sums of money from Support Systems and putting even their business at risk of collapse. Indeed she was stunned. But the news that he had fought his addiction and was still dealing with his compulsion by attending GA meetings made her think better of him. Even so, she blamed herself for not keeping a closer eye on the firm's finances, because, had she discovered what Drew was up to sooner, she might have been able to stop him gambling before matters had got quite so out of control. 'Does Caroline know about any of this?'

'I've been too ashamed to tell her. Hasn't she borne enough without learning that I've now wrecked her life and the kids' by gaming away everything that matters to them?' Drew muttered heavily. 'I'm behind with the mortgage payments, too.'

Abbey was frantically trying to work out where she could get money from to pay off his outstanding debts, but she was paying a mortgage on her apartment as well. Furthermore, at a time when the financial markets were weak, interest rates were high and house prices were falling, it was not a good plan to seek to remortgage in the hope of clearing some surplus cash. 'I don't know what to say or do…'

'There's nothing you can do. I've ruined our lives.'

'You have to tell Caroline. She's going to find out and it would be kinder if she heard it from you first,' Abbey told her brother and watched his eyes slide away from hers in instant dismay at that daunting prospect. 'Surely she already knows about the mortgage on the house?'

Drew hung his head and released his breath in a hiss. 'I forged her signature on the application.'

Abbey said nothing. She was way beyond exhibiting shock and voicing angry disapproval and was much too busy worrying about the ultimate result of Drew's financial depredations on the firm. She went back into her own office with the account books and, in between studying them and eventually tracing the evidence of Drew's unauthorised cash withdrawals, she sat staring into space. Caroline would be distraught. What if the business went down as well? Belatedly recalling that Nikolai was expecting her to join him to view the house he was planning to buy, she headed out to meet him.

Nikolai registered that something was wrong with Abbey within minutes of her appearance. There was a hollow look in her eyes and her usual pizzazz was noticeably absent. He was still annoyed with her. Women were usually eager to please him and he had learned to take that treatment for granted. But Abbey wouldn't make the required effort and he could only take that as an insult when he compared her attitude to what he had gathered about her former behaviour with her late husband. He knew that he could call on any number of beautiful attentive women, who would not hesitate to fulfil his smallest request. Had he not been engaged in a pretence with Abbey designed to dupe the press, he would have dumped her by now, he assured himself grimly.

Mr bin Hashim greeted them and left them alone to explore the big house. Abbey wandered around in Nikolai's wake with all the energy and sparkle of someone attending a funeral. Undeniably the property was vastly superior to anything she had shown him earlier that week and the entertainment suite and pool area in the basement were nothing short of spectacular.

'Perfect for parties,' Nikolai remarked.

Abbey's delicate profile froze, as she was picturing naked beauties frolicking in the clear water and displaying their perfect bodies for his benefit. She had seen the way other women looked at him at the premiere and it had shocked her. He might as well have a bullseye painted on his back, for he was a target for predatory women. He was gorgeous, young and fabulously wealthy and generous. She had no real hold on him and she had never been so aware of the fact. She was, after all, just one of the herd and lower than most in her ranking, for their apparent relationship was ninety-per-cent bogus to fool the media, she reminded herself dully.

'I'm very impressed that you pulled this off for me, *milaya*,' Nikolai confided huskily, closing an arm to her spine and folding her close with the easy intimacy that could still catch her unawares. He was a very physical guy. She was tempted to rest back into his arms and lean on him like the sort of weak, needy female she would never allow herself to be.

'Have you any advice to offer me with regard to the country property?' she pressed instead.

'Do you ever stop thinking of work? You look very tired,' he censured.

The lawyers would negotiate and tie up the purchase of his new London home. In the back of his limo, Nikolai turned to her and handed her a jewel case. 'A tribute to mark your efficiency,' he murmured smoothly.

Abbey froze. 'You're already paying me handsomely for concierge services. Nothing else is required.'

'I always reward excellence, *lubimaya*.'

Abbey flipped up the lid of the case to discover an exquisite gold watch studded with diamonds and marked with a famous designer name. She wondered if he was rewarding her excellence in bed or her excellence as a concierge. The reflection ate into her self-respect like acid and shamed her. 'It's beautiful. Thank you,' she said stiffly, because she knew he wouldn't take it back and was reluctant to offend him yet again.

To please him, she fastened the watch to her wrist, where it sparkled prettily in the sunlight coming through the window.

'The limo will return to pick you up at seven. We'll dine out,' Nikolai announced when the car drew up outside her apartment building.

Hopefully, her new wardrobe would have been delivered while she was out. Sveta had dispatched one of Nikolai's domestic staff to wait at her apartment and unpack the garments when they arrived. When Abbey walked into the hall, the first thing she noticed was the distinctive meow of a cat. She studied the pet carrier sitting by the wall. A gift card was attached to the carrier and it bore Nikolai's bold signature.

Filled with curiosity, Abbey knelt down and unlatched the door. A seal point Siamese kitten strolled out and turned almond-shaped vivid blue eyes on her and Abbey's heart just melted on the spot. An envelope full of information and a pedigree from the breeder was also attached to the carrier. Abbey petted the playful kitten, wondering how on earth Nikolai had guessed that she had always dreamt of owning a Siamese. It was a wonderful surprise at the end of a truly hideous and distressing day.

Later, when she had managed to set the kitten down for a few minutes, she phoned Nikolai direct to thank him. 'She's adorable...totally adorable,' she chattered with warm enthusiasm. 'I can't thank you enough.'

Nikolai was interrupted in the middle of a board meeting, and his lean dark face was slashed by a slow smile of satisfaction. He liked to excel in every field and his competitive spirit had been challenged by her lukewarm response to his other gifts. 'You like her? Her blue eyes are as bright as yours.' Across the boardroom table Sveta was staring at him in surprise and he turned his handsome dark head away. 'What will you call her?'

'Lady...she's incredibly elegant. You won't object if I bring her over to your apartment tonight, will you? I couldn't leave her home alone on her first night! Did you pick her personally?'

'Yes, I did. When she hissed and tried to scratch me, I knew I'd found the right one!' Nikolai smiled and hoped Abbey never found out just how much that little ball of fluff, purchased from a leading breeder, had cost him. He was well aware that she was choosing to approve this particular present because a kitten came without sinful gold-digging associations attached.

Abbey selected a green cocktail dress with a full skirt from the vast new wardrobe that had overflowed into her guest room and slid her feet into strappy sandals with high heels. She was wondering whether or not she ought to offer Drew the ten thousand pounds she had in her savings account. A greater emergency might yet lie ahead, not least the current cash-flow problem with the business, and she wanted to be sensible. She decided to hang on to her savings in the short term and tried not to think about the vast amount of money that her brother had wasted while he pursued his gambling addiction. That cash was gone now and not all the wishing in the world was going to bring it back.

CHAPTER NINE

'WHAT are we going to do about Drew's debts?' Caroline whispered in a despairing tone, her voice still hoarse from the constant crying she had done in recent days.

'I don't know,' Abbey replied honestly, drained by the stress of trying to calm and support her friend through the family crisis. 'But I've done the sums. Right now—assuming there's no new disaster waiting in the wings to jump out on us—the business is at least bringing in enough cash to pay your regular outgoings and your home is safe.'

'We can't even sell it to settle the debts. We owe more than the house is worth,' Caroline lamented. 'I can't live like this.'

'I know that you're scared and that you feel that Drew has let you down—'

'Drew's had a lot to bear in other ways.' Caroline cast a speaking glance down at her wheelchair. 'But even though I'm not the woman he loved and married any more, he's never once complained. Maybe the gambling was an escape from the pressure of living with me.'

Abbey made no comment. She had no idea what had got into her brother and did not feel qualified to hazard a guess. Drew had always been quiet and sensible, and dangerous, thrill-seeking behaviour like compulsive gambling seemed out of character for him. But Abbey had only to look at her own conduct in recent weeks to accept that people often acted in unpredictable ways and not always for any clearly defined or rational reason. How, after all, could she explain her own total obsession with Nikolai? Was it a physical infatuation that would fade?

'You could ask Nikolai Arlov for a loan.'

Abbey's bright auburn head jerked up in dismay at that unwelcome suggestion. Caroline's oval face was pale and strained and her shadowed eyes were pleading.

'I *couldn't*,' Abbey replied curtly. 'That's out of the question.'

'Why not? I mean, the bank wouldn't even consider us in the state we're in, but Nikolai might as a favour to you.'

Abbey was furious with Caroline for even broaching the subject. 'Fixed as we are for finance right now, it would take us a lifetime to pay Nikolai back. And if I asked him to give us money it would be like *selling* myself to him!' Abbey proclaimed, compressing bloodless lips and almost shuddering at the idea. Of course she had thought about asking Nikolai for help, of course she had, but she didn't see why he should be expected to settle her brother's debts for him. And she cherished the truth that she had never looked on Nikolai or treated him like an open wallet. She was not greedy like his previous lovers and she knew he valued that difference.

'Don't be so fanciful,' her sister-in-law argued. 'Nikolai seems to delight in spending money on you. He never stops buying you expensive gifts and you're already practically living with him! Everyone reckons that what he has with you is much more than a casual affair.'

Everyone? Not Abbey, however. She stared out into the back garden where Alice and Benjamin were playing on the swing set. Every so often one of the twins cast an anxious look back towards the house, revealing that both children were aware of the tension in their home. Abbey hurt for her nephew and niece, who'd had to contend with a lot of parental rows and grief over the past fortnight. She wished she had a magic wand to wave that would make all the trouble and strife go away, but she didn't.

'Nikolai and I...well, it's not like you think,' Abbey argued uncomfortably, wishing she could tell the other woman about Nikolai's desire to fool the press into believing that he was involved in a serious relationship with her. Only then would Caroline understand how hollow Nikolai's apparent attentiveness really was at heart.

Caroline gave the younger woman an unimpressed glance. 'Isn't it? You've been here thirty minutes and he hasn't phoned yet to maintain contact and I'm surprised. Over the last two weeks I doubt if you and Nikolai have been apart for longer than a couple of hours.'

Abbey dropped her head, knowing that that was the truth. The even more disturbing truth was that she had revelled in every minute of that intense togetherness and had discovered a happiness she had not known she was capable of experiencing. Happiness for her was falling asleep in Nikolai's arms at night and waking up still in them.

'And that's not the way he usually behaves with women according to the articles I've read,' Drew's wife contended. 'He's a cold customer as a rule and yet he's bought you a fortune in diamonds, is having you driven around in your own personal limousine and he marches you out everywhere he goes.'

'I returned the diamonds to him,' Abbey reminded Caroline and, catching sight of the time, she frowned. 'Look, I'll have to go or I'll get caught up in the traffic—'

'And be late, which Nikolai detests. He's got you dancing to his tune all right. It's hard to credit that only a week or so ago you were heartbroken about Jeffrey and Jane Dalkeith.'

Abbey's face shadowed, as she recognised the slight hint of scorn in that unnecessary reminder of her lowest hour. After the shock of Jeffrey's betrayal had sunk in, she had adapted fairly quickly and she had no quarrel with that assessment. 'Well, I had to get over that, didn't I? I wasted too many years grieving for Jeffrey to waste any more time agonising over a past that I couldn't change and a man who never loved me the way I loved him.'

'Very sensible. I only wish you would practise some of that sense around Nikolai.'

'Common sense died the day I met him,' Abbey quipped on the way out and she wasn't joking when she said it. Something stronger than she was had drawn her to Nikolai and forged links she couldn't break or walk away from.

The limousine ferried her back to Nikolai's penthouse apartment where she had spent a great deal of the last fortnight. Lady, more at home there than she was at Abbey's apartment and thoroughly spoiled by the attentive domestic staff, danced up to Abbey playfully in the hall to greet her. Abbey smiled and scooped up the Siamese kitten to cuddle her. When she reached the bedroom with the overnight bag she had brought she undressed and went for a shower. It was her last night with Nikolai, at least the last night of the two weeks she had agreed to spend with him, and who could tell what would happen next? Would she even see him tomorrow? She had no idea.

Nikolai never mentioned the future and never referred to anything more than a week in advance. Bearing that nerve-racking truth in mind, Abbey did not understand how it had come about that *she* could not picture a future without *him*. She could scarcely accuse him of having encouraged such delusions. Yet, a thousand memories bound her to him now. He filled every corner of her existence and most of her thoughts. He phoned her all the time. He gave her flowers and gifts every day. He listened to her when she talked. He had escorted her to parties, clubs and dinners and in his company time flew. She was getting used to the designer clothes, the diamonds and the endless pursuit of the paparazzi. She was getting dangerously accustomed to having Nikolai in her life.

She lifted a fleecy towel to dry herself before massaging rose-scented oil into her skin. Workwise, the past weeks had been less successful. She had so far failed to fire Nikolai's interest in any of the country properties she had researched and, even though Drew's financial problems and the fallout from that revelation had proved a source of continual worry for her, she had found comfort and forgetfulness in being with Nikolai.

He was the tough guy who had never had an indoor pet until Lady came along as a regular house guest. Nikolai talked much more freely about his background now. For the first nine years of his life he had been cared for and indulged. He had attended a private school and had shared the many privileges that his grandfather had enjoyed as a leading diplomat. But the older man's sudden death from a heart attack had ended that life for ever and had catapulted Nikolai into the custody of a bullying father, who had never wanted him, and a step-mother who despised him. As heir to his grandfather's substantial estate, Nikolai had been violently resented by his birth father's family. When Nikolai was finally hospitalised for the injuries inflicted on him by his rela-tives, his father had decided it would be safer to banish him from the household altogether and he had fostered out his illegitimate youngest son to a poor family in one of the toughest estates in St Petersburg.

'That experience and those years made me what I am today,' Nikolai had insisted fiercely. 'I learned how to rely on myself and how to fight my own corner. After I completed my military service I educated myself for the business world.'

The very bareness of his later childhood had touched Abbey's compassionate heart to the core. She knew exactly what had made him tough and unyielding. He had never known a woman's love and tenderness as a boy and the experience of violence followed by hunger and poverty had brutalised him, before a soldier's training and the horrors of war had made his reserve even more impenetrable. Yet she had watched him play with the tiny Siamese kitten with a gentleness that fas-cinated her. This was the same guy who held her close in the aftermath of passion and let her smother him in kisses. She adored him and it was precisely because she adored him that she would not ask him to bail her brother out of trouble, for that single act would throw up the barrier of his great wealth between them. She was convinced that it would also erase any suggestion that they might be equals and destroy his respect for her.

Nikolai respected her independence and her refusal to grab at all the material things he could offer her. She wore the clothes and the jewellery because he insisted, but when he ended their affair she would leave those expensive trappings behind her, for the last thing she would want would be the reminders of what had been. She climbed into a filmy bra and knicker set and smoothed pale lace-topped stockings up her very long legs. Mischief sparkled in her eyes. The two weeks might be over, but she wanted him to regret the fact, not celebrate the prospect of his renewed freedom.

On the drive back to his penthouse Nikolai studied the tabloid gossip page Olya had given him. It included one of the official photos he'd had taken of Abbey and himself at the party he had thrown days earlier.

Abbey looked spectacular in a green satin dress that showed off her glorious hourglass shape as well, its décolleté neckline displaying the diamonds he had draped her in. Speculation about their relationship was now rife in the British media. The paparazzi were following their every move. There were already rumours about the house purchase and her involvement in its selection. The word *inseparable* was being thrown about with great abandon. And, in truth, during the past fortnight, Nikolai had managed to spend a good part of every day and all of every night with Abbey. *And* with Lady.

His sardonic mouth quirked with amusement. Abbey and her kitten, Lady, were truly inseparable because Abbey, for all her steely efficiency, was a total pushover for her tiny pet. He had watched her get out of bed during the night without complaint to comfort the lonely animal when she'd cried, and strive to meet her constant demands for attention. It had struck him that Abbey would make a terrific mother. It was easy to imagine her with a baby in her arms and the very fact he *had* imagined such a thing for the first time in his life with a woman had seriously spooked Nikolai. He had got in too deep. It was time to back off.

He was happy to admit that the nights had been amazing and that his hunger for her voluptuous body had yet to abate. Between the sheets, for all her innocence at the outset, she had proved to be a fast learner, who was surprisingly willing to fulfil his every fantasy. Indeed, sexually she was gradually surrendering her inhibitions to become his perfect match. He enjoyed showing her off as well. Abbey was *his* in a way no other woman had ever contrived to be—an intelligent partner, who could talk on a business level, and a stimulating companion who never bored him. He thought he would miss her when there was no longer any need for their pretence. He had yet to muster the interest to look out for her replacement in his bed, a lack of forward planning which was most unlike him.

The one aspect of Abbey's nature that he knew he would not miss, however, was her reserve. Throughout their time together he had been aware that something was amiss and that she was seriously worried about that something, but despite the many opportunities he had given her she had steadfastly refused to confide in him and, indeed, had continued to infuriate him by insisting that nothing was wrong. Nikolai did not appreciate being treated as though he were stupid. He had always believed that it was a man's fundamental right and responsibility to look after his woman, but it was not a role that Abbey seemed willing to extend to him. He had no doubt that her late husband, Jeffrey, had enjoyed more preferential treatment.

And he knew that Abbey's attitude was influencing his own, because although he had that morning received an extraordinary visit from the Greek tycoon, Lysander Metaxis, Nikolai had no plans as yet to share the amazing content of what had been discussed with Abbey. Was it even remotely possible that he could be related to an Englishwoman? For about the tenth time Nikolai brought up a photo of Lysander's wife, Ophelia, on his laptop and studied her with a frown. She was very small and blond and pretty. Physically there was no resemblance whatsoever. It was most probably a wind-up, not a deliberate one, of course, for Metaxis was not the joking type, Nikolai acknowledged wryly. But someone somewhere might well have got their wires crossed and screwed up the investigation into the history of Ophelia's troubled mother. Even so, Nikolai was still keen to go to the party Lysander had invited him to this evening and interested in meeting Lysander's wife and looking over the documentation that had been mentioned.

A gift bag in one hand, Nikolai strode down the corridor to the bedroom where he knew Abbey would be waiting for him. After a day apart from her he could never resist the need to immediately reacquaint himself with the allure of her warm, willing body and, after being carried off to the bedroom or ambushed on the sofa day after day, she had given up trying to interest him in food and good conversation when he first came through the door. When he saw her standing across the room, her glorious body fetchingly attired in sexy green lingerie, he was entranced. Setting the gift bag down by the bed, he moved towards her.

'Nikolai.' Abbey turned round the minute she heard the door open. Her violet eyes were luminous, her soft full mouth settling into a radiant smile. He still stole the breath from her body every time she saw him. It wasn't humanly possible for him to get more gorgeous but her response to him never lessened. In a spectacularly elegant Italian designer suit, his lean, darkly handsome visage roughened by a faint masculine shadow of blue-black stubble, he looked stunning from the brilliance of his dark golden eyes to the sensual slant of his beautiful mouth.

'You look really hot, *lubimaya*,' Nikolai husked, running his smouldering gaze over her with bold appreciation.

Nikolai reached for her without hesitation, folding her slim, shapely body into his with sensual thoroughness. He found her generous mouth and kissed her with a slow erotic skill and hunger that sent heat hurtling through her quivering length like a fizzing firework of energy. He turned her round, long fingers curving across her stomach to ease her hips into contact with his erection. As a whimper of sound left her lips, he lifted his hands to caress her breasts through the fine fabric of her bra, catching the pink-topped peaks between thumb and forefinger to tease them to prominence.

'Tell me why is it that when I had you only this morning, I still spent the entire day fantasising about coming home to have you again?' he breathed in a hoarse undertone.

'I don't know,' she said when she could get her voice to emerge levelly again, although she could have told him, had she felt sufficiently generous, that she'd reacted to him the same way.

'You're an addictive habit,' he murmured, unhooking her bra and stripping it away.

A gasp escaped her as he moulded his hands to her full breasts. The straining peaks were very sensitive. He continued to explore her while she watched him in the mirror. There she was poised like a doll to be undressed in his arms, enslaved by desire and longing. She didn't like the image or the thought, for both hurt her pride.

Nikolai studied their reflection in the same mirror with a thrill of fierce satisfaction; he had tamed his haughty beauty and she was his now to enjoy. An arm curved round her narrow waist, he sent seeking fingers down to the junction of her pale slender thighs. He skimmed over the slippery surface of her panties, feeling her body leap with response, the shiver that racked her against him and finally the heat and damp below her mound that telegraphed her readiness.

'It's been a wonderful two weeks,' he conceded, shimmying down the panties over her hips and slowly lifting her free of them, every single move, every single glide of his expert fingers calculated to increase her craving a thousandfold.

Abbey tensed. That was his first reference to the fact that their agreement as such on where she slept was almost over. It wasn't much for the basis of a relationship, she thought wretchedly, but it was all they had as a framework. Nikolai swept her up into his arms and down onto the bed.

'Did I mention that we're going to a party tonight?' he murmured.

'No...' Abbey wasn't pleased, for she had been

looking forward to spending an evening at home with Nikolai and enjoying his undivided attention. 'And I haven't brought anything with me to wear either.'

'I'll take you home first to get changed. But you'll definitely need the diamonds. Our hosts are Lysander Metaxis and his wife, Ophelia.'

Abbey's lashes fluttered as she focused on his darkly handsome face above hers. 'I've seen him in the business pages of the newspapers—'

'His wife looks like a Botticelli angel,' Nikolai remarked, poised at the foot of the bed and shedding his clothes in a careless heap.

It was unusual for Nikolai to compliment another woman in her presence—he was far too clever with her sex to make mistakes like that. And Abbey discovered that she was insecure enough to experience a stab of jealousy about a woman she had never met. She studied Nikolai, her attention pinned to his muscular, hair-roughened chest and long, powerful thighs while she marvelled at how natural it felt to be with him now. He came down beside her and she ran appreciative hands over him. The hot pulse at the heart of her and the groan of satisfaction he emitted urged her on. She loved to touch him and revelled in his response. While she had no idea what went on in his head, she had a much better grasp of what he liked in bed.

Nikolai knotted his hand in her tumbling curls and vented a driven groan of tormented pleasure, a long, deep shudder racking his long, powerful length before he hauled her up and rolled her over onto her back. 'I've been thinking of this all afternoon, *milaya moya*—'

'I thought nothing came between you and business.' Abbey was trembling with excitement as he spread her thighs and slid between them.

'Except you.' His need for her at a torturous height, Nikolai stared broodingly down at her, wondering what it was about her that got under his skin to such an extent, wondering what insanity had taken hold of him when he had gone to the effort of buying the contents of the gift bag by the bed.

Mollified by the assurance, Abbey let her head roll back on the pillow, her slender neck extending. He rocked against her and she lifted her hips to receive him. He plunged into her silken depths with a husky growl of masculine pleasure. 'I'll make it last, *zolotse moya*,' he swore.

And he did, driving her up to the heights with his slow, sure movements, where she splintered into a hundred pieces of sobbing delight. But it wasn't over, for no sooner had she recovered from that first climax than he turned her over onto her stomach and took her again. This time he shifted the pace up tempo and set a hard, insistent rhythm that made her cry out in an agony of abandon and raw excitement. His passionate possession overwhelmed her and there were tears in her eyes when he turned her back to face him again. Exultant dark golden eyes raked over her hectically flushed face.

'*Bihla dika*...that was wild,' he breathed appreciatively, and he buried his face in the damp valley between her heaving breasts before kissing his way up to the delicate skin at the side of her neck.

Abbey's head was swimming, her body tingling from the aftermath of sweet, drowning pleasure. All around her, the world seemed to have slowed down and she felt detached from it and ridiculously happy with Nikolai's arms round her. In fact just then she never wanted to move again. Nikolai nuzzled at her neck and she felt the slight nip of his sharp teeth and made no complaint. She knew she had probably left scratch marks halfway down his back: she had got carried away, too.

'You can't go to sleep. We're going out,' Nikolai reminded her cruelly, literally lifting her off the bed and carrying her into the shower with him.

'It'll take me for ever to do my hair!' Abbey complained, not wanting to go anywhere when she felt such a mess, particularly not to a party presided over by a woman with the face of a Botticelli angel.

'I could have a hairdresser called in—'

'It's not that simple—'

'If you would let me take care of you, it's *always* that simple!' Nikolai declared with supreme confidence.

Ten minutes later, Abbey was unwinding the towel from her damp hair when she saw the bruise marring her pale throat. A smothered shriek of horror erupted from her as she peered at her reflection in the vanity mirror above the sink. 'Oh, my word, what have you done to me?' she gasped, touching the blue-black bruising that now marked where he had employed his teeth. 'I thought only teenagers did stuff like this!'

A towel anchored round his lean bronzed hips, Nikolai studied her neck with a disbelief akin to her own. He could not believe that that one tiny nip could have inflicted such highly visible damage. Dark blood flared over his cheekbones. He was equally stunned by his own lack of control and forethought.

'Do you have vampires in Russia? Are you in training?' Abbey demanded. 'I can't go out with a love bite on my neck! People will laugh at me.'

'Won't make-up conceal it?' Nikolai prompted a tinge desperately.

'Nothing I have will cover *that* up.'

'Get ready. I know what will cover it—'

'I'm not going to the party, Nikolai.'

'I am. With or without you,' he responded without hesitation. Lysander Metaxis had most effectively roused his curiosity. 'But I would much prefer to have you by my side.'

Engaged in combing her wet hair, Abbey blinked back the hot moisture suddenly stinging the backs of her eyes since his declaration that he would go to the party alone if necessary had startled her, as well as rousing the fear that the end of their affair was already within view as far as he was concerned.

She switched on the hairdryer despite thinking that getting ready to go out was a waste of time because she could see no way that she could be made presentable enough to appear in public. He went to get dressed. When she joined him an hour later she had done her make-up and straightened her hair into smoothly acceptable curls and pulled on a pair of jeans.

'Our evening meal awaits us and the solution to my...' Nikolai struggled to find a suitable word '...thoughtlessness,' he selected, bending down to scoop up Lady, who was playing with his shoelaces.

Purring like a car engine revving up, the Siamese was deposited back down again before she could shed hair on his suit. The kitten tried to persuade him to lift her again and wound her sleek body round his ankles like a crying fur muff. Abbey lifted the noisy little animal to comfort her.

Abbey was stunned when she realised what Nikolai's solution to the love bite entailed. A decidedly superior jeweller and his assistant awaited them in the main re-

ception room with a choice of jewelled collars. A magnificent pearl collar with a sapphire clasp was selected
to encircle her neck and cover the bruise. She was still
fingering it uncertainly when she took a seat at the
dining table to eat.

'You're not seriously buying this just to cover the
mark up, are you?' Abbey pressed in dismay.

'The subject is closed,' Nikolai told her loftily.

'As long as other people can't see it, I don't mind. In
fact you're forgiven. A love bite is a sort of rite of passage,
isn't it?' Her eyes danced with belated amusement. 'And
I did miss out on the experience when I was younger.'

'You always strike me as very young,' Nikolai
admitted. 'You have a quality of freshness and naïvety
that you'll probably never lose.'

Abbey was still thinking about the statement when
they walked into her apartment. Did he find her im-
mature? Unsophisticated? Gullible? How big a strike
against her was that quality? Already having decided
what she would wear, she rifled through the built-in
wardrobe in the guest room until she found the short
gold metallic dress she sought. The dress was bang on
trend in colour and style and very elegant worn with
oyster shoes that reflected the shade of the breathtakingly conspicuous pearl collar.

The paparazzi took so many flash photos as they
emerged onto the street that she was bedazzled and
blinking frantically when she climbed into the limousine.

'I meant to give you this earlier.' Nikolai handed her
a gift bag as they drove across the city to the party.

Abbey extracted several small items carefully wrapped
in tissue paper. The first package produced a miniature
horse that was dressed in medieval war tack. A frown line

pleated her brows. The second item she unwrapped was a doll's house doll, a distinctly handsome black-haired male dressed like a Crusader knight about to go into battle and armed to the teeth with little metal weapons.

'Nikolai...this is incredible,' she whispered in fascination.

'There's no man in your doll's house. Someone must have fathered the tribe of kids in the attic.'

'Where on earth did you get him from?'

'The Kensington Doll's House Festival.'

'I had planned to go but I couldn't find the time,' Abbey confided, stunned by the gifts and setting her warrior onto his horse where he looked most at home and very impressive. She would not have dreamt of telling Nikolai that, while her fatherless doll's house family might inhabit a medieval castle, he had got the time frame wrong for the interior and the inhabitants were more staidly set in the Victorian age. And she was dumbfounded that he had chosen to attend such an event purely to buy her presents. A third package yielded a minuscule silver dressing table set that was exquisite and a skilful miniature landscape painting. 'Wow...I'm astonished. Thank you very, very much.'

'I was amazed by the quality of the craftsmanship.'

'You're much too generous,' Abbey told him uncomfortably.

'I enjoy giving you stuff. I don't have a family to spoil like other men,' Nikolai pointed out.

That observation warmed and touched her, but it was to be the last pleasant moment in a challenging evening. When they arrived at Lysander and Ophelia Metaxis's spectacular town house, they were personally greeted by their hosts. Abbey was immediately aware of her hostess's keen interest in Nikolai. The tiny exquisite blonde, who was unquestionably a beauty, bubbled over with warmth and chatter from the instant she laid eyes on Nikolai and greeted him with breathless enthusiasm. A cold presentiment of trouble slid through Abbey like ice trickling into her tummy. Lysander Metaxis was equally gracious in his welcome. Indeed, amidst the exchanged glances, companionable chuckles and general air of bonhomie shared between their hosts and Nikolai, Abbey felt very much like an outsider, marooned on the edge of a charmed circle.

Abbey told herself off for being silly and over-sensitive. When had she become so jealous and possessive that she couldn't handle Nikolai enjoying the company of an attractive woman? But on more than one occasion during the evening that followed, it seemed to Abbey that Nikolai's gaze regularly strayed in an effort to pick Ophelia Metaxis out of the crush. He was quiet as well, his manner preoccupied. An hour later, Abbey turned round and discovered that Nikolai appeared to have vanished and that there was no sign of their hostess either.

As she walked out of the beautiful ballroom towards the hall Lysander Metaxis strode forward to intercept her. 'Ophelia is showing Nikolai our art collection. Didn't he mention it?'

'Maybe I didn't hear him…' Abbey stared up at her tall, classically handsome host, who seemed to find nothing odd or worthy of comment in his wife's behaviour with Nikolai.

'I'm sure they'll be back soon. Let me get you a drink,' he murmured smoothly, cupping her elbow to guide her back into the ballroom.

Some time later when Abbey was striving to work up

an appetite for the delicious spread of food being served at a buffet, she received a call on her mobile phone. When she answered it, her face froze in dismay at the onslaught of Caroline's sobbing hysterical voice.

It took Abbey several minutes to calm her sister-in-law down enough to understand what the other woman was trying to tell her. When she did work it out, she was very much shocked: earlier that evening, Drew had been attacked in the staff car park by a couple of men and beaten up. Her brother was in hospital.

'I'll be with you as soon as I can get there,' Abbey promised, her heart hammering out her tension. 'Did you call the police?'

The police had gone to the hospital but Drew was refusing to make a statement. That information confirmed Abbey's worst fears. Evidently Drew believed the attack was linked to his gambling debts and he was afraid to make a formal complaint. She called to order a taxi to pick her up. Its arrival alerted Lysander Metaxis to Abbey's planned departure and brought him to her side, just as she sent Nikolai a text telling him that she was leaving the party because her brother had been hurt. She explained the situation to her Greek host, apologised for leaving early and politely ignored his suggestion that she wait to consult Nikolai on her next move. Just at that moment, Abbey didn't care if she never laid eyes on Nikolai Arlov again.

Her phone started ringing as she was getting into the taxi, but when she realised the caller was Nikolai she switched it off. She had had a lousy, humiliating evening and she was in no mood to pretend otherwise. The first half of the party Nikolai had virtually ignored her, the second half he had performed a disappearing act with another woman. Clearly, Abbey was no longer flavour of the month on Nikolai's terms and she was feeling horribly hurt and betrayed at a time when she believed she should only be thinking about her brother's plight.

CHAPTER TEN

DREW was a mass of cuts and bruises. Tears sprang to Abbey's eyes when she saw her brother's puffy face and black eyes. He had a couple of broken ribs and he had lost a front tooth. 'Oh, Drew...' she framed unevenly, reaching for his limp hand where it rested on the bedclothes.

Stationed at the other side of the bed in her wheelchair, Caroline gave her husband's sister a stony look. 'Maybe you could have prevented this from happening,' she condemned.

Abbey was pale as death and her strained eyes were haunted, but she lifted her chin in receipt of that comment. 'No. Drew's the only person who could have prevented this. Please don't start redistributing the blame.'

In his hospital bed Drew nodded affirmation of that speech and then groaned at the pain induced by the movement. 'My fault...*all* my fault,' he stressed, looking anxiously at his wife.

'Did you tell Nikolai?' his wife asked Abbey, scrutinising the luminous pearls and the dress that had turned heads from the instant Abbey had arrived at the hospital. 'Didn't he offer to come here with you?'

'No. He was busy elsewhere when you called so I came in a taxi.' Abbey sat down by the bed, her tummy turning queasy as she finally allowed herself to wonder what Nikolai had been doing with his hostess. But just then didn't seem the right moment to deal with the bewilderment and pain steadily building inside her and she thrust such thoughts aside to look levelly at her sister-in-law. 'Nobody's going to sort this out for us, Caroline. This is our mess.'

'If you cared about your brother, you would at least have asked Nikolai to help,' Caroline declared tautly.

'No, Caro,' Abbey's brother interrupted, his discomfiture patent. 'That's not fair.'

'We don't have any other options unless we try to sell the business,' Caroline muttered brokenly. 'And where's that going to leave us all?'

Conscious of her brother's disquiet at the discussion that had broken out, not to mention the hostile edge between his wife and his sister, Abbey decided that by staying at the hospital she was acting as more of a hindrance than a help. She stood up and asked Caroline if she needed her assistance in any other way. In receipt of a frosty negative, she departed, wondering if her friendship with the other woman would ever recover from the recent blows that had been inflicted on it.

When she got back to her apartment she set the miniature warrior on his war horse outside the castle on her hall table and touched his black hair fondly with the pad of her index finger. She didn't think her little medieval hero was ready as yet for the culture shock of bathrooms and floral wallpaper that awaited him in the doll's house. Suddenly tears were spilling freely down Abbey's weary face and she went into her bedroom and removed the pearl collar.

Studying herself in a wardrobe mirror, she covered the bruise on her neck with splayed fingers and wondered frantically how she and Nikolai could have so swiftly lost the warmth and passion they had shared during the early part of the evening. Somehow she had missed out on the signs of him losing interest. She hadn't realised it would happen so fast or so brutally. But then, nothing she had ever read about Nikolai had suggested that he went in for long-term relationships, so really the ultimate end result had been staring her in the face all along. She had just been too weak to face that, too trusting to toughen up and prepare herself for the hurt on the horizon. It felt like the worst possible moment to admit to herself that she had fallen madly in love with her Russian billionaire. What was the point of knowing that now when he was gone? And how was she supposed to cope with an ongoing working relationship with him in the future?

Would he still expect her to continue the pretence that they were involved in an affair as per their secret agreement? When had everything become so complicated? Why was she still thinking about herself rather than her brother? The attack on Drew had just been a warning to him and his family. There might well be worse to come when no further cash was forthcoming. Her skin turned clammy. She felt as if her whole life were falling apart. She undressed and removed her make-up and pulled on the T-shirt and shorts she usually slept in. All week she had got accustomed to sleeping in nothing more than her skin and cuddling up to Nikolai when she got cold. Already those memories felt like memories from another time and place and, as such, inappropriate.

Around one in the morning, the doorbell buzzed. Lying sleepless in bed, Abbey switched on the lamp and got up. She peered through the spy hole in the door at the tall black-haired male waiting outside. It was Nikolai. Raking restive fingers through her tangled copper curls, she unlocked the door.

'I've got nothing to say to you,' she told him flatly.

'I've got plenty to say,' Nikolai growled, settling cold dark eyes on her and pressing the door wider with a determined hand. 'You just walked out of the party and went to bed like nothing had happened?'

'What did you want me to do? Make a big scene? Chase after you? Stage a search of the Metaxis house for you?' Abbey slammed back as she stepped back to let him in, reluctant to risk disturbing her neighbours with an argument on the doorstep.

'Anything would have been preferable to just walking out on me!' Nikolai thundered back at her in an icy rage. 'That was rude and unpardonable!'

'So was abandoning me for the Botticelli angel woman halfway through the evening!'

His lean, handsome features tensed. 'Don't call her that,' he censured. 'And I did *not* abandon you. How did you think I felt when I found out your brother was in hospital?'

Abbey shrugged an uncaring shoulder, affronted by his defence of Ophelia Metaxis from even a flattering label. She studied him and gritted her teeth, determined not to surrender to her emotions. In Nikolai's radius such a loss of control would be a terrible weakness. He had discarded his bow tie and undone his shirt. An angry flush accentuated his high cheekbones. She had never seen him so furious, for it was very rare for Nikolai to gave way to his emotions or to allow them to show on the surface. 'Who told you?'

'Lysander, and he also told me which hospital Drew was in. When I got there, your sister-in-law, Caroline, had the good sense to explain the situation to me. I couldn't believe that I had to hear it from her rather than you!' he shot at her in a raw undertone, condemnation stamped in every hard angled line of his lean, strong face.

Embarrassment and confusion attacked Abbey in a debilitating surge. 'I didn't think my family's problems had anything to do with you,' she told him defensively.

'Of course they have. You're part of my life. Have you any idea how I feel knowing that, even though your brother has been beaten up, you were still refusing to ask me for help?' Nikolai launched at her wrathfully.

Abbey wound her restive hands together in an anxious movement. She didn't really understand why he was so angry. 'It wasn't your problem,' she responded.

'But it was yours and your problems should be mine!' Nikolai slung back at her with unquestioning conviction. 'That's what I'm here for, isn't it? When you're in trouble, you should share it with me and come to me for help!'

Abbey was stunned by the sound of that very traditional masculine assumption emerging from Nikolai. He made it sound so simple, so straightforward. He was outraged that she had not confided in him and she was taken aback by the realisation that her silence about her brother's predicament could have struck Nikolai as both an insult and a form of rejection. 'I didn't know that you would feel like this about it. I just didn't want to be one more woman in a long line who tried to take advantage of your wealth...'

'Would it have hurt your precious pride too much?' Nikolai demanded with derision.

'I thought you liked my independence,' she muttered.

'Your independence, but not your folly. Something might have happened to you. You were threatened and you didn't even tell me that. If you had been hurt in any way, I'd have killed them,' Nikolai growled with chilling bite. 'But I have only one more question to ask you…'

Lashed by his fury, Abbey was trembling, wondering how she could have miscalculated so badly. 'And what is that?'

'Would you have excluded Jeffrey from all knowledge of your brother's dilemma?' Nikolai asked bluntly.

Abbey felt her face freeze, for she knew she would never have kept Jeffrey in the dark. But six years ago she had been a good deal younger and less self-sufficient and theirs had been a different relationship, one in which her trust was based on the fact that she believed Jeffrey had made a commitment to her because he loved her. 'That was different.'

Nikolai paled beneath his bronzed skin, his strong facial bones taut and clenched. He was still light-headed with anger and disbelief. She didn't trust him and her refusal to even ask for his assistance had hit him like a sudden punch in the stomach. He was done with striving to measure up to the late husband she had once idolised, he told himself hotly. He would live in no man's shadow and he would be no woman's second-rate substitute.

'I can't believe you're so annoyed with me. I didn't want to ask you for money, particularly as I can't see how a loan that size could ever be repaid the way things are at present,' Abbey admitted uncomfortably.

'I've arranged for the debt to be settled. I was impressed that your brother had confessed his addiction and was already attending Gamblers Anonymous. I believe he's learned his lesson,' Nikolai confided. 'The money isn't a loan and I don't require repayment. Consider it a gift.'

'I can hardly turn it down when you've offered it to Drew and Caroline on those terms. It's their business now. You've taken the whole matter out of my hands.' A gift? Abbey felt that she had already accepted far too many gifts. 'You're being incredibly kind and generous—'

'Forget it,' Nikolai cut in starkly.

'I presume I'm still working for you—'

'And everything else, *lubimaya*,' Nikolai drawled, closing a lean hand over hers and tugging her up against him before she could guess his intention. She swayed against him, her knees as weak as the rest of her with simple shock.

It seemed she had got totally the wrong end of the stick. She could not credit that a male who saw her only in terms of a casual affair would consider it his right to share her worries and solve her problems. Nikolai was offended because she had not turned to him for help. Nikolai, it seemed, would be happy for her to be needy and clingy if it meant he could step in like a knight in shining armour and save the day for her. A dazed smile on her lips, she rested her buzzing head on his shoulder and thought about how much she loved him and of how worthy he seemed of her affection at that moment. Her suspicions about the level of his interest in Ophelia Metaxis were completely allayed by the concern and support he was demonstrating. She recalled the nonchalance of Ophelia's husband, Lysander, and castigated herself for getting jealous without good reason. The tide of relief washing over her made her feel weak and incredibly tired.

'You're falling asleep.' Nikolai sighed, bending down to lift her up into his arms and carry her back to her bed.

'It's been a long night,' Abbey mumbled, settling into the mattress like a rock embedding in soft sand. And that was her very last memory until she wakened the next morning.

Nikolai watched her sleep. It was a small bed and he didn't want to disturb her when she was so tired. He knew he should have told her what had happened at the party. He knew he should have explained, but his news would keep until tomorrow when she had recovered the energy to listen and stay awake.

Having dimly assumed that Nikolai was staying the night, Abbey was surprised to open her eyes and discover that she was alone. She had slept like a log but something had woken her up. The doorbell? The phone? She flinched when both went off almost simultaneously. She scrambled out of bed, picked up the cordless phone and threw on her dressing gown to answer the door. She was too flustered and sleepy to check the spy hole first and it was an unpleasant shock to find a paparazzo brandishing a newspaper outside and asking her for a comment.

'A comment on what?' she queried as she pressed the answer button on the phone just to stop it ringing.

The man held up the newspaper page right in front of her eyes. Abbey put out a hand and snatched it out of mid-air to peer down at the photo with incredulous force.

'Don't answer the door until you've talked to me,' Nikolai told her over the phone. 'There's a crazy story in the papers this morning.'

It was a photo of Nikolai on a balcony with a woman and the woman had her arms wrapped round him. Abbey recognised Ophelia Metaxis's golden curls and her white-and-silver evening gown. The picture must have been taken with a telephoto lens from the garden the night before. 'You bastard,' Abbey whispered strickenly and she pressed the phone's disconnect phone button with violent force.

'Would you like to talk?' the paparazzo asked hopefully.

Abbey slammed the door in his face. The phone was ringing again. She banged the disconnect button again. What an idiot she had been to trust Nikolai, to assume he was innocent rather than guilty, to refuse to accept that the most obvious explanation was usually the right one! Maybe Lysander and Ophelia Metaxis had one of those trendy open relationships she had read about, for she could not see any other explanation for Lysander's complacent attitude to the sight of his wife blatantly seeking out another man's company. Particularly a man with a reputation as notorious as Nikolai Arlov's. She showered and dressed quickly, selecting a tailored black pinstripe suit from her wardrobe and teaming it with a purple fitted top. She had to knot a scarf round her neck to hide the bruise there.

Two members of Nikolai's security team were waiting in the foyer downstairs to clear her passage through the crush of camera men waiting outside. The limo driver handed her a phone before she could even get into the car. It was Nikolai once more. 'Don't you cut me off again,' he warned her with scorching emphasis.

In the mood that Abbey was in, that order was like waving a red flag in front of a bull. She depressed the disconnect button with a punitive finger and passed the phone back. There were no further calls during the drive to his apartment. Abbey was in a rage that she continued to stoke higher and higher. Anger was a welcome block for the pain that she didn't want to acknowledge or experience. Had Nikolai left her last night to meet up with Ophelia somewhere?

Why hadn't he just told her it was over? The affair, the pretence, *everything*! That was the problem, Abbey conceded fiercely, the pretence that they were engaged in a serious relationship had expanded until it had taken over her entire life and convinced even her that it was real. But Nikolai dealt more in fact than fantasy and she had to face the truth—the messy public ending to their affair was very much Nikolai, who had not hesitated to ditch his last lover at his late father's memorial service. She supposed the truth was that he didn't care; he only cared about what *he* wanted. And yet, last night, Nikolai had seemed to care about her and her family very much, a little voice reasoned at the back of her head. He had seemed sincere.

But then Jeffrey had always seemed sincere, too, Abbey conceded wretchedly, bitterly. Her late husband had lied to her and cheated on her and she hadn't suspected a thing! Obviously she was not very good at sussing out liars. Possibly she was not very good at understanding men either. But she was determined not to allow another man to make a fool of her. She was going to tell Nikolai what she thought of him. How shabby could a guy be? Disappearing with the hostess at a very well-attended party? If he had wanted out, he should have said before it hit the newspapers and humiliated her.

Nikolai was in the hall when she arrived. Her gaze lit on him like the dart of a flame and then cloaked as she mentally shut a door against his stunning dark good looks. 'You have a very hot temper, *lubimaya*,' Nikolai drawled. 'Think before you lose it because Lysander and Ophelia are here and I do not think I will easily forgive you for making us both look stupid.'

Abbey was thrown badly off balance by that opening speech, for she could think of no circumstance that could reasonably explain the presence of both Lysander and Ophelia Metaxis at his apartment at nine o'clock in the morning. 'What on earth is going on?' she demanded shakily.

Nikolai closed a hand over hers. 'Ophelia and I have just had DNA tests taken. We suspect that her mother may also have been mine,' he shared tautly. 'If it's true, it's a discovery that would mean a great deal to me.'

Abbey's fingers were almost crushed in the tense grip of his. That astonishing statement plunged her into a state of bewilderment. 'DNA tests for siblingship?' she prompted. 'You think that you and Ophelia Metaxis might be related by blood?'

'We hope so. Lysander and Ophelia tracked me down. Lysander came to see me yesterday and shared the evidence he had found. Together we were able to piece together the most likely explanation for the events that culminated in my birth over thirty years ago.'

'You think that Ophelia may be your sister?' Abbey's brain was functioning extremely slowly. It was a challenge to take on board any facts which, on first hearing, struck her as beyond the bounds of credibility. 'But surely that's very unlikely?'

'Before my grandfather put my father out of his life, he apparently used his influence to get his son a junior diplomatic position in the embassy in London. I was not aware of the fact that for several years my father and his family lived here. During that period he sent my half-sister, Feodora, to an exclusive English girls' school,' Nikolai advanced as he walked her into the elegant drawing room with its spectacular views. 'That's where Feodora met Ophelia's mother, Cathy.'

Ophelia Metaxis sprang up from a sofa with the bubbling energy that characterised her and extended a photograph to Abbey. 'I found this photo in my mother's personal effects.'

Abbey stared down at the black-and-white snap of a strikingly handsome man who bore a strong resemblance to Nikolai. 'Is this your father?' she prompted, turning it over and striving without success to read the name scrawled on the back of it.

'Yes. Kostya Arlov,' Nikolai supplied. 'Feodora was willing to confirm certain facts. She and Cathy became friends, and Feodora twice had Cathy to stay with her in London. My father had few moral scruples. He wouldn't have thought twice about seducing a school-girl. She was only seventeen…'

'And very impulsive,' Ophelia piped up wryly.

'But this long after the event we can only guess at what happened between them. Feodora remembered feeling envious of the attention her father gave to Cathy and she was able to confirm that Cathy disappeared from school several months later, supposedly suffering from glandular fever. Of course she had fallen pregnant. I was born in a private clinic and handed straight over to my father,' Nikolai continued. 'But his father—my grandfather—was not prepared to allow me to be adopted out of the family.'

'My maternal grandmother, Gladys, would never have allowed my mother to keep an illegitimate child.

The whole matter was hushed up and buried, and I'm afraid my mother died a long time ago,' Ophelia explained. 'I only found out that I might have an older brother recently and it's taken a great deal of detective work to get us this far.'

'We have already discovered that, like Ophelia, I, too, share our mother's rare blood group,' Nikolai murmured, closing a hand to Abbey's spine and drawing her beneath the shelter of his arm.

'What must you have thought when you saw that photo of us on the balcony last night?' Ophelia commented with a grimace.

'You were rather inconsiderate last night,' Lysander Metaxis scolded his wife with a frown.

Ophelia gave Abbey an apologetic look. 'I'm sorry, Abbey. I was gasping to meet Nikolai and too impatient to be polite about it. Then once I got him all to myself, I got very emotional telling him about Mum and my sister, Molly, and I started to cry and he hugged me.'

'I don't think I'll tell you what I thought,' Abbey confided, drawn by Ophelia's natural warmth, her own defensive rigidity evaporating. 'I knew something was going on between all of you—'

'And Abbey always thinks the worst of me,' Nikolai imparted above her head.

'No, of course I don't,' she argued for the sake of appearances, but she knew his accusation was the truth.

'We'll have the DNA results in a couple of days,' Lysander Metaxis pronounced with a note of finality.

'I know already. I don't need tests!' Ophelia proclaimed with irrepressible conviction. 'I know now in my heart that Nikolai is my brother.'

Lysander and his wife took their leave and Abbey did not accompany Nikolai to the hall to see them out. She was trying to be tactful and she had a lot to think about. Everything she had assumed when she saw that tabloid photo of Nikolai and Ophelia together had been knocked on its head and shown to be nonsense.

'Why didn't you tell me who Ophelia might be before we went to their party?' Abbey questioned when Nikolai reappeared.

'Why didn't you tell me that your brother and you were being threatened by thugs?' he riposted.

'That was a little different. I thought if I told you about it, you would think I was asking you for financial help and I didn't feel comfortable with that,' Abbey answered truthfully. 'I was too proud.'

His lean bronzed face was taut. 'I said nothing because I thought there would be no real substance to Ophelia's belief that we were related—'

'Nor were you prepared to admit how important it was for you to find out who your mother was,' Abbey guessed.

'That, too. I always assumed that my mother must have been a prostitute,' Nikolai revealed, shocking her with that blunt admission. 'In the days when I knew him, my father was well known for consorting with hookers.'

Abbey could read in his brilliant dark eyes how much that belief had troubled him and her heart swelled inside her. Indeed it was only with the greatest difficulty that she restrained herself from rushing across the room to wrap comforting arms round him.

'But a schoolgirl, his own daughter's friend,' Nikolai added with a disgusted shake of his handsome dark head. 'Kostya was a nasty piece of work. Ophelia's mother went on to lead a very troubled and unhappy life. Being forced into early motherhood and having to give up her child at that age would have done nothing to help.'

'I'm sorry I thought the worst about you and Ophelia.' Abbey felt light-headed with relief that all her worst nightmares had failed to come true.

'I don't mess around with married women and you should have known that.' Nikolai closed a hand over hers to urge her in the direction of the hall. 'Now that we have that sorted out, we have a busy day ahead.'

Abbey had nothing noted down in her diary. 'Have we?'

'But you'll have to go home and change first. I'm afraid that you're not dressed for the occasion.'

'Not more diamonds, surely,' Abbey muttered uneasily.

Nikolai laughed out loud at the note of dismay in her voice. He paused to tug down the scarf at her throat and press his expert mouth to the bruise there with a slow, sensual flourish. 'Who knows what the day will bring? But I'd love to see you wearing something feminine and summery.'

At the touch of his lips, gooseflesh flared at the nape of her neck. She gazed up at him, marvelling at the potent masculine appeal of his lean, dark, handsome face, her attention lingering to admire the black curling ebony spikes of his lashes and the astonishing beauty of his brilliant dark eyes. 'What's the occasion? Where are we going?' she asked.

'It's a surprise.'

'Is it work or play?'

Nikolai banded her close with possessive hands and the proximity of his lean, hard body sent arrows of sexual awareness darting through her slim body. 'I don't think I've ever looked on you as work and you're too demanding to fall into the other category.'

'But we're still faking a serious relationship, aren't we?' Abbey wanted to remind herself of that salient fact to keep her feet securely anchored to the ground.

Nikolai raised a sleek brow. 'The jury's still out on that one.'

'No, it's not,' Abbey told him in the lift. 'We're faking.'

Just when she wanted him to argue, Nikolai made no comment. He dropped her home and arranged to pick her up again within the hour. The paparazzi took several shots of her smiling face as she got out of his car. She wondered where on earth he was taking her and chose a floral tea dress from her wardrobe, teaming it with elegant high heels and the pearl collar to cover the bruise on her throat. While she was doing her make-up her brother, Drew, phoned her from hospital and told her how generous Nikolai had been and how very grateful he was.

Ophelia phoned her as well before she went out again to invite her and Nikolai to dinner at their home that weekend. Abbey was embarrassed, not knowing how to say that she and Nikolai were not such a couple that she could accept or decline invitations on his behalf. She said she would mention it to him, and would very much like to have known how Nikolai had described her status in his life to his potential sister.

A perfect blue sky and bright sunshine greeted Abbey when she left the limo at a private airfield and boarded the helicopter which Nikolai was to fly. Fierce curiosity assailed her: she could not think where in the world they might be going and conversation above the noise of the rotor blades was impossible.

Abbey was quick to take in the view when finally

Nikolai drew her attention to it. Registering that their journey was clearly coming to an end, Abbey noticed that they were flying over a very large expanse of roof. Nikolai turned the helicopter to head for the landing pad and only then did Abbey appreciate that the property below them was a moated and battlemented castle set in beautiful grounds. She assumed it was a hotel.

Vaulting down onto the ground in advance of Abbey, Nikolai scooped her out of the helicopter with enthusiasm. 'I like the dress... I will never tire of looking at your legs.'

'Where are we?' Abbey demanded.

'Berkshire. Cobblefield House.'

Abbey recognised the name and tensed. 'What are we doing here?'

'I told Sveta to arrange a viewing.'

Abbey literally gnashed her teeth at that announcement. She had worked night and day and trailed round all the estate agencies in search of the elusive country property that would ignite his interest and she had got nowhere! She had seen the details of this same property two weeks earlier and had immediately discounted it from her list of possibles because it contained none of the luxury extras that Nikolai was accustomed to finding in his various homes round the world.

'But it's a medieval castle,' she pointed out tartly.

'The heart of the house may still be, but the building was considerably extended and renovated in the nineteenth century.'

'And hasn't been touched much since then. If I'd known that you liked this sort of place, I could have shown you several,' Abbey pointed out, furious that she had had no idea that he would even consider a historic listed house as a potential base in the country.

But Nikolai failed to rise to the bait of that feminine reproach and strode forward to greet the man crossing the lawn towards them. They were ushered into a fascinating, if cluttered, interior in which many generations of the same family had each left their mark. Their guide was the owner and he was selling up lock, stock and barrel because he had no heir. Abbey was quick to admire the massive fireplaces, the very grand oak staircase and the beautifully shaped mullioned windows. The reception rooms were large and gracious and full of light and the same historical charm and sense of elegant proportion ensured that the bedrooms were equally pleasing to the eye.

'What do you think of the house, *milaya moya*?' Nikolai enquired as they walked round the walled garden where box-edged borders of roses rioted with glorious romantic abandon.

'Well, it's not exactly tailor-made for you, is it?' Abbey quipped. 'The bathrooms can be counted on one hand. The last modernisation programme ended before the First World War and, because it's a listed building, alterations will be a complex issue for there are a lot of restrictions.'

'Are you always so practical?'

'You're paying me to look out for your interests and warn you of the pitfalls,' Abbey reminded him.

Lean, strong face taut, Nikolai expelled his breath with an audible hiss and turned her round. He looked down at her, his shapely hands enclosing her wrists. 'Did you like the house?'

'Yes, *I* did, but I can't see you falling into ecstasies over the quality of the wainscoting and the holes left in the walls by the Cromwellian attack.'

'There's no accounting for taste,' Nikolai murmured huskily, lowering his handsome dark head to taste her generous mouth in an explorative kiss that made her shiver, heat flowering low in her stomach. 'We're staying in a local hotel tonight. It's time to leave.'

'Why aren't we going back to London?'

'I have my reasons.'

Thirty minutes later they were walking into a magnificent country house hotel and Nikolai was ordering dinner.

'It feels strange to be anywhere without paparazzi,' Abbey confided. 'Do you know I haven't got so much as a toothbrush with me?'

Nikolai sent her a flashing smile of amusement. The suite was large, opulent and extremely comfortable. Wonderful flower arrangements scented the rooms. Champagne was served when Abbey reappeared after freshening up as best she could in the marble bathroom. She sensed Nikolai's tension and it bothered her and made her wonder what was wrong.

'Just one more diamond,' Nikolai murmured softly, extending a small jewellery box to her.

'*Another?*' Abbey exclaimed in dismay, flipping open the lid, and then freezing to stare down at the huge diamond solitaire ring. 'What am I supposed to do with this?'

'You really are making this a challenge.' Nikolai sighed. 'I couldn't get down on one bended knee and keep my face straight, but I always assumed that most women are programmed to recognise an engagement ring at first glance.'

Abbey's smooth brow indented. 'It's an engagement ring?' she gasped in shock.

'Will you marry me?' Nikolai asked, tugging the ring out of the box and trying to put it onto the wrong finger.

'Oh, my gosh…*yes!*' Abbey told him, extending the correct finger to be helpful.

'You don't want time to think about it?' Nikolai checked, his dark gaze liquid with emotion as he studied her.

'What's there to think about?' Abbey whispered in a wobbly voice as shock began setting in hard on her and tears clogged her throat and stung her eyes like mad. 'I love you loads.'

'Do you?' Nikolai was staring down at her hard enough to strip paint. 'So why are you crying?'

'I'm so h-happy!' Abbey hiccupped.

Nikolai was holding on tightly to both her hands as if he was working up to saying something. A muscle jumped at his tense jaw line. 'I meant it when I told you I'd never felt like this before. I didn't even realise what love was until I fell for you—'

Abbey squeezed his hands. 'You fell for me?'

'A head-on collision. Crash-bang-wallop, as you Brits would say,' he mocked. 'I was so jealous of what you felt for Jeffrey.'

Abbey was studying him wide-eyed. 'You…*were?*'

'It drove me crazy.'

'I was just a teeny bopper when I loved Jeffrey. It was different,' Abbey admitted ruefully, freeing one of his hands to reach up and trace the angle of one hard masculine cheekbone, rejoicing in her freedom to touch him. 'You should appreciate the fact that I fell for you, warts and all! You paraded all your faults and I still managed to love you.'

'What faults?' Nikolai fielded.

Abbey rested her palm on his shirt front. 'I don't think we should go there tonight. You know, I'm not perfect either. I was just trying to point out that even though you bribed me into dining with you on our first date and I knew that was very wrong, I still fell head over heels in love with you.'

Nikolai covered her hand with his. 'I had to fight just to get time with you and then I took advantage of you that first night and knew I would pay for it—'

'Of course you took advantage,' Abbey said ruefully, knowing that Nikolai would always make the most of any opportunity to get what he wanted. He was built that way and aggressively set on winning and nothing would change him.

'You hated me for it,' Nikolai growled. 'It wasn't worth it.'

'I have one question I have always wanted to ask. And you must be honest. Sveta, Olya and Darya— what's the score there?' Abbey enquired gently.

'I founded a business school in St Petersburg and I offer jobs to the top graduates. They're terrific workers. Sveta and I grew up in the same neighbourhood. I have never slept with any of them,' Nikolai completed with an honesty that she found compellingly attractive.

'But I'm not sure I could accept them staying with you, because they all want you,' Abbey responded with equal frankness.

'I'll deal with the situation,' Nikolai asserted. 'I promise.'

Abbey looked at the ring glittering on her finger and curved her arms round his neck. 'How long have we got before dinner?'

A wolfish grin slashed his sculpted mouth as he read her expressive face. 'Long enough, *lubimaya*,' he asserted, bending down to lift her and carry her through to the bedroom.

Happiness was racing through Abbey like an ongoing electric shock. She still couldn't quite credit the ring on her finger and the idea that she was loved. 'I thought you only committed to sex—'

'You made me want much more. I wanted to be the very special guy that you had the worthy, important relationship with. I'm hopelessly competitive,' Nikolai teased. 'Why do you think I gave you that file on Jeffrey?'

Abbey stiffened and pulled a face. 'That was awful, but I was glad I finally found out.'

'That was the night I realised I loved you, because I felt like such a bastard for hurting you like that. I was really worried about you, as well.'

'I think I shifted from lust to something more that night as well. You were very caring,' Abbey confided, planting a kiss on the corner of his mouth as she wrenched off his tie and attempted to extract him from his suit jacket.

'Is this lust or love?' Nikolai's eyes were bright with wicked amusement.

'Does it matter?'

Just then it didn't. Nikolai claimed her mouth with feverish hunger and for quite some time there was no sensible conversation whatsoever. Clothes were discarded in careless heaps. Passion blazed between them. He made love to her with all the natural fire of his temperament, but there was a new tenderness in their joining. Afterwards she was in tears of happiness again. Suddenly her whole world seemed drenched in sunlight and she was full of bright hopes for the future.

'What made you pick Cobblefield House?' Abbey

whispered curiously while she still lay in his arms, but carefully arranged so that she could continue to feast her gaze on her glittering engagement ring.

Nikolai groaned out loud. 'Didn't it remind you of anything?'

Bemused by the question, Abbey shook her head.

'The centre portion looks like your doll's house...'

Her eyes opened very wide. 'Oh, my word...is that why?'

'My inspiration...didn't you realise that's where I got the idea that you liked Siamese cats?'

'Lady,' Abbey sighed comfortably. 'She was one terrific present. I love that little cat to bits—'

'When I saw you with the kitten, I thought you would make an amazing mother,' Nikolai confessed. 'For the first time ever, I thought of becoming a father without freaking out and I realised that you were different.'

'I'm not sure I'm ready to be a mother yet,' Abbey admitted. 'I'm only just adjusting to the being engaged, and then getting married and living in a giant castle.'

'I love you. I'll wait. Whatever makes you happy,' Nikolai intoned.

Abbey gave him a radiant smile. '*You* make me happy,' she told him with supreme confidence.

'Stay still, darling,' Ophelia Metaxis urged her three-year-old daughter as she adjusted the focus on her camera. 'I want to get a picture of you beside your baby cousin.'

Little, blond, dark-eyed Poppy was stationed beside Abbey, who was holding her infant son, Danilo, on her lap. The baby, black-haired and blue-eyed, dressed in his magnificent christening robe and shawl, was fast asleep.

'He really is gorgeous,' Ophelia remarked and she

patted her slightly protruding tummy. 'I hope my next is a boy.'

At Caroline's request, Abbey settled Danilo on her sister-in-law's knee for another set of photos for her side of the family. The DNA tests had been positive: Ophelia and Nikolai were half-brother and sister, the children of the same mother, Cathy. Ophelia had told Abbey about her little sister, Molly, who had been adopted when Ophelia was a teenager. Nikolai was as keen as Ophelia to track down Molly, but so far their enquiries had failed to establish any leads.

Two years had passed since Abbey and Nikolai had got married. Lysander and Ophelia had staged the wedding for them at Madrigal Court, their beautiful Tudor country house, which lay only thirty miles from Cobblefield House. The wedding had been a fantastic day, which had served to wipe out all Abbey's unhappy memories of her first tragic wedding day. Now she lived very firmly in the present with her attention centred squarely on the husband she adored and her first child.

Caroline and Drew were a good deal happier than they had been, for they had more time to spend together as a family. Nikolai owned a share of Support Systems now, and Olya managed the business, ensuring that expenses never got out of hand and everything ran like clockwork. Darya was based in New York and still working for Nikolai, as was Sveta, who had taken charge of Arlov Industries in London. Nikolai had other very presentable St Petersburg business graduates working for him, but none of them ever seemed quite as dangerously adoring and possessive of their handsome employer as the original threesome.

Abbey's miniature doll's house castle had been rearranged and refurbished as a more suitable home for a medieval knight. The lady of the house now wore a Tudor bed gown and there was a hip bath by the fire with her fanciable husband inside it. Abbey reckoned that a warrior just home from battle would probably need a good wash. She believed that the moment Nikolai confessed to having attended the Kensington Doll's House Festival to buy her presents was the same moment that she should have worked out that he loved her.

She was amazed by how well Nikolai had settled down into being married, as she had initially feared that he might find it boring to be with one woman. But she had gradually come to understand that, deep down inside, Nikolai must always have craved the ordinary stability of a home and a family that he could depend on being there for him. She knew that he loved coming home to her at the end of a long day and that he found the household routine soothing after the volatile cut and thrust of the business world. When he had to travel on business, he phoned her continually to keep up with every little detail of her life while they were apart.

'I never realised how much babies slept,' Nikolai remarked, leaning down to jiggle his son's tiny feet in unashamed hope of waking him up.

'I'm going to put him up to bed for a nap. He's had so much attention he's exhausted. If you wake him, he'll be as cross as tacks and he'll cry and cry and cry. On your head be it,' Abbey warned, settling Danilo into his father's arms.

Looking a touch daunted by that forthright speech, Nikolai carried his four-month-old son carefully upstairs to the nursery with Alice, Benjamin and Poppy all trailing in their wake. The children all liked Nikolai because he played with them and read stories. He was refreshingly natural and comfortable with children, and Abbey was convinced that he would be a wonderful father to their child, since he took his responsibility towards his child seriously. She watched him settle their infant son into his cradle with infinite gentleness and her eyes prickled with responsive tears of appreciation.

Sometimes she loved Nikolai so much, it almost hurt. She felt incredibly blessed to have found him and won his love.

As the children scampered noisily downstairs in advance of them Nikolai caught his wife to him and kissed her with a slow, deep, erotic thoroughness that she found incredibly exciting. 'I'd love to tell everyone to go home just so that I can have you all to myself, *lubimaya*,' he confided gruffly.

'I love you,' Abbey whispered dizzily, her arms wrapped round his neck, 'but we can't chuck our guests out just so that we can go to bed.'

Nikolai pressed her close and stole another passionate kiss, scanning her flushed and beautiful face with tender intensity. 'Can't we?'

'If we switched the heating off, that would probably clear the house faster than a fire alarm,' Abbey commented abstractedly, clutching the lapels of his jacket to stay upright.

'It would probably get rid of me, too.' Nikolai laughed with a suggestive shiver, for there was snow on the ground outside.

'Oh, I could keep you warm,' Abbey told him languorously, her turquoise violet eyes filled with love and contentment.

Nikolai dealt her a deeply appreciative smile because
he did not doubt that statement for a moment. 'I think
I love you more every day I'm with you, Mrs Arlov.'

Abbey reached up to kiss him again, and it was some
time before they went down to rejoin their guests with
the excuse that Danilo had refused to settle...

HIRED: FOR THE BOSS'S PLEASURE

She's gone from personal assistant
to mistress—but now he's demanding
she become the boss's bride!

Read all our fabulous stories this month:

MISTRESS: HIRED FOR THE BILLIONAIRE'S PLEASURE
by INDIA GREY

THE BILLIONAIRE BOSS'S INNOCENT BRIDE
by LINDSAY ARMSTRONG

HER RUTHLESS ITALIAN BOSS
by CHRISTINA HOLLIS

MEDITERRANEAN BOSS, CONVENIENT MISTRESS
by KATHRYN ROSS

www.eHarlequin.com

HPE0209

REQUEST YOUR FREE BOOKS!

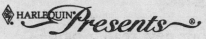

2 FREE NOVELS
PLUS 2
FREE GIFTS!

YES! Please send me 2 FREE Harlequin Presents® novels and my 2 FREE gifts (gifts are worth about $10). After receiving them, if I don't wish to receive any more books, I can return the shipping statement marked "cancel". If I don't cancel, I will receive 6 brand-new novels every month and be billed just $4.05 per book in the U.S. or $4.74 per book in Canada, plus 25¢ shipping and handling per book and applicable taxes, if any*. That's a savings of close to 15% off the cover price! I understand that accepting the 2 free books and gifts places me under no obligation to buy anything. I can always return a shipment and cancel at any time. Even if I never buy another book, the two free books and gifts are mine to keep forever.

106 HDN ERRW   306 HDN ERRL

Name _____ (PLEASE PRINT) _____

Address _____ Apt. # _____

City _____ State/Prov. _____ Zip/Postal Code _____

Signature (if under 18, a parent or guardian must sign)

Mail to the **Harlequin Reader Service:**
IN U.S.A.: P.O. Box 1867, Buffalo, NY 14240-1867
IN CANADA: P.O. Box 609, Fort Erie, Ontario L2A 5X3

Not valid to current subscribers of Harlequin Presents books.

Want to try two free books from another line?
Call 1-800-873-8635 or visit www.morefreebooks.com.

* Terms and prices subject to change without notice. N.Y. residents add applicable sales tax. Canadian residents will be charged applicable provincial taxes and GST. Offer not valid in Quebec. This offer is limited to one order per household. All orders subject to approval. Credit or debit balances in a customer's account(s) may be offset by any other outstanding balance owed by or to the customer. Please allow 4 to 6 weeks for delivery. Offer available while quantities last.

Your Privacy: Harlequin Books is committed to protecting your privacy. Our Privacy Policy is available online at www.eHarlequin.com or upon request from the Reader Service. From time to time we make our lists of customers available to reputable third parties who may have a product or service of interest to you. If you would prefer we not share your name and address, please check here. ☐

HP08R

HARLEQUIN *Presents*

HARLEQUIN *Presents*

kept for his
Pleasure

She's his mistress on demand!

Wherever seduction takes place, these fabulously
wealthy, charismatic, sexy men know how to
keep a woman coming back for more!

She's his mistress on demand—but when he
wants her body *and soul* he will be demanding
a whole lot more! Dare we say it...even marriage!

CONFESSIONS OF A
MILLIONAIRE'S MISTRESS
by Robyn Grady

Don't miss any books in
this exciting new miniseries
from Harlequin Presents!